I0831178

THE BAR IS IN HELL

THE BAR IS IN HELL

a novel

JOSHUA MURRAY

DOG NAMED DOG
PRESS
NEW YORK

Published by Dog Named Dog Press
Islip Terrace, New York

Interior design by Joshua Murray

First Edition March 2026

ISBN 979-8-9997774-0-9

For Jess,
who keeps me grounded.

My eyes fail with tears,
my heart is troubled,
my liver is poured out on the ground.

— **Lamentations 2:11**

"A rich man is nothing but a poor man with money."

— **W.C. Fields**

1

SOMETHING WAS DRIPPING DOWN THE walls, and Dan didn't know what it was. He didn't care. The only thing he cared about was getting out of these handcuffs. He'd been on his knees for hours, and all the earlier pins and needles in his legs were replaced by a deep radiating hurt in the center of his bones. His thighs were on fire, and his ankles were stiff from the cold concrete floor—and all he could do was watch the walls drip.

One of Fat Jackie's goons got him good, right across the face, the sight of the gun catching him with a slice above the eye. The blood streamed steadily at first, but was mostly dried now and leaked slowly down his cheek. His hand was killing him, and the throbbing made the restraints so tight his whole arm pulsed with his heart-beat. It was stupid, trying to dislocate his thumb like that. And it didn't even help. In a movie he saw as a kid, Stallone and Antonio Banderas were driving around in the rain or some shit, and that was how Antonio escaped his cuffs—a quick pop, a slight grimace, then he was free. Goddamn movie magic.

And Jackie's goons were still laughing at him.

The taller one with the eyebrows was crying, he was laughing so hard, hand on his hip, making a real show of it. The shorter one with the boots chuckled silently with his arms folded over his fat fucking stomach—Jackie picked a pair of gems with these two assholes. It was a hell of a way to spend Ash Wednesday.

Fat Jackie opened the door, the metal scraping against the dirty, wet concrete. Why were the walls weeping? Dan felt like he was in an Edgar Allan Poe story, half expecting Jackie to be carrying a raven or a big jug of wine with ropes coiled around the base. Jackie took the gun from Eyebrows and walked over, still chewing on that same goddamn toothpick he'd had pinched in his mouth since yesterday—now with a chunk of ash in the center of his fat fucking forehead. God, what was Dan thinking doing that to his hand? What was he going to do? Fight these two dipshits and escape? Find a way to get to Jackie, and what, what then? Shoot him?

Jackie walked across the room, tapping the gun against the side of his thigh with each step, his face fading to darkness in the spaces between the dim hanging lights, naked and buzzing, until he stood looming. Dan, stuck on his knees looking up at Jackie, Jackie down at him, the barrel of the gun hovering inches from Dan's mouth, a smirk on Jackie's dumb face like the first scene of some POV porno. The only thing missing was the reflection of a ring light in Dan's eyes and a black couch. He wasn't scared of guns being waved in his face anymore. That stopped being scary around the third time it happened that day. Now everything just felt over-dramatic. The coldness of the steel did feel nice against his head, though.

"Dan-A-Plenty. Long time no see," he said.

Dan did his best to keep his voice steady, acting calm and unfazed. He didn't have much power on his knees, all beat up and bound, but fuck Jackie—getting under his skin was the only play Dan had left.

"Has it—how long have I been down here?" No one answered him. "Not long enough for you to get any new jokes. Hey, Eyebrows, hand me the remote, I've seen this one before."

Jackie laughed mockingly to emphasize his insincerity. "There he is, Dan-A-Plenty," he turned to his goons. "He's got plenty of jokes, plenty of comments, and plenty of schemes. You always got something cooking, don't you, kid?" Dan sighed and closed his eyes. He hated it when Jackie called him *kid*. "As long as I've known you. Since high school. What was that one? The first one. You came to me for money, senior year, you remember, with the candy bars? You thought you had it all figured out back then, too, kid. Twenty years later, and what's changed? Not a damn thing."

"Stop it with the kid shit. You're three years older than me, Fat Jackie."

"It's just Jackie."

"Try looking from this side."

Jackie took the gun away from Dan's forehead and jammed it under his chin. "You think I'm fucking around here, asshole? Where is my money?"

"If I didn't have it yesterday, I don't have it today."

Jackie kicked Dan in the stomach, knocking him

off his knees, flat to the ground. "You've got bite for someone who owes me ten thousand dollars. I want it back."

When the air came back into Dan's lungs, he coughed out, "I'm working on it."

"You were working on it when it was seven grand. Now it's ten. Time to pay up."

The cool ground felt so refreshing on his face that Dan could almost have gone to sleep right there. Maybe that was blood loss.

"What do you care about ten grand, man? That's like, what? That's...it's nothing."

A white-hot flash of pain shot through Dan's body, turning his vision neon pink and speckled with stars. Fat Jackie was squeezing his hand and twisting it around backwards. Dan let out a scream before he even realized it.

"It is nothing. To me. I spent six times that yesterday because I was bored of my car. But to you, it's a lot, and it's still my money." He let go of Dan's hand. "Do you have any more smart-ass comments?"

"Just one."

Jackie pressed his foot onto Dan's cheek—wet dirt and grit smearing across his face.

Dan aimed his words carefully. "You were a fat fucking asshole in high school," he said. "And you're a fat fucking asshole now."

Face red and seething, too angry to form words, Jackie lifted Dan by the armpits, spraying spit with the effort. His breath came out in snorts like a pig, wheezing out his exhales. He pushed Dan into his goons, and they turned him back to face Jackie. They each grabbed an elbow and put a hand up between their face and Dan to shield themselves from the spray.

Shit.

Jackie huffed over, arm's-length away, and pointed his gun in Dan's face. His thugs turned their bodies from Dan and tried to cradle their ears to their shoulders to protect themselves from the pop. It was the first time since getting snatched from his bed that Dan felt afraid—Eyebrows and the other one kicking in his door at the motel, a plastic bag over his head. If Dan hadn't sweated it all out, he probably could have pissed himself.

Shit.

"Fuck this, you're not worth it. You never were." Fat Jackie pulled the hammer of the gun back with his thumb and turned his face away.

"No wait!" Dan cried out.

Dead silence. The water dripped and trickled down the wall, each drop filling the room until it was suffocating, sucking out the oxygen, and burying them in echoes. Dan's breathing and heartbeat flooded his ears, the blood rushing through his drums. The wheeze at the end of Jackie's breaths sliced the air like the crack of a whip. Dan's vision narrowed to a pinpoint, and the world lost color. Everything was slow, and Dan watched the movements in the room before his brain could make sense of them.

Jackie's finger was curled around the trigger.

The silence of the room was shattered, and everyone flinched.

Dan let out a gasp.

"Goddamnit, hold on," Jackie said, his voice thick with annoyance. He lowered the gun and reached into his pocket—his cellphone blaring out its default ringtone.

He flashed the screen to Dan and his thugs. "It's the ex. Always the worst fucking times." He slid his thumb across the screen and lifted it to his ear. The men let go of Dan, and he collapsed to his knees, retching, but nothing came up. They were laughing again. The metal scraped across the wet grit as Jackie pulled the door closed behind him, leaving his two assholes just chuckling away. Dan rested his forehead on the ground and gasped wildly for all the air left in the room.

"I don't blame you," Eyebrows said. "That was a close one. I didn't know which way he would go. I think he was actually going to do it this time, don't you?"

The shorter one nodded.

Eyebrows continued. "Normally, I can tell, but he had that same look in his eyes—the one he had with, what was his name?"

"Georgio," the short goon said, crossing himself mockingly. "My hearing was fucked for weeks. Blood got in my ear and was sloshing around. What a shit show."

Dan's mouth tasted like copper, and his lips trembled—he tried to hide it from the two henchmen as he straightened up and stretched his legs so he could sit flat on the ground. His knees were killing him, and his thighs were burning, an ache pulsing through his lower back like Jackie was tap dancing on it. Hell, maybe it'd be worth a bullet right through his fucking face right now, end it all. *Fuck it,* he thought.

A flood of embarrassment washed over Dan as he wondered why, then, was he so scared of Jackie pulling the trigger. He was going to. Dan couldn't explain how he knew, he just did. It was in the air. The room vibrated with it like Dan stumbled into a den of rattlesnakes. He always had a hard time respecting Jackie—it was impossible to be scared of someone he'd seen change in the corner of gym glass, all red and bashful—but this wasn't that kid, this was someone different. Dan could take just about any amount of punishment and spit it right back in Jackie's fat face out of spite, but a bullet through the bridge of his nose was a different story. Dan might have really stepped in it this time. His nerves filled his mouth with sand, and Dan was tempted to run his tongue over the ground to collect water from the wet cement, just a drop to soothe his thirst.

Jackie came in, phone still to his ear, and the door moaning that horrible sound. He waved the gun casually between the three of them with the flick of his wrist, and the two men lifted Dan by his armpits to the same position they were in before.

"Uh, huh," Jackie said to the person on the other line. He took the phone from his ear and circled it around his temple. *She's crazy,* he mouthed with an eye roll and put the phone back to his cheek. "Uh, huh. No, I'm listening. I heard you! She's fine. No, no, I'm saying—hey, *I'm saying*—I'm *sure* she's fine! No, be—because we raised her right. Oh fuck off, no, absolutely not. I did too. Don't say that. Okay, you're right, no, shut up, you're right." He rolled his eyes again. "Like last time, yeah yeah, I agree. What? I said I agreed. What tone? She does this, you know that." Jackie rubbed his gun hand across his forehead, pinching his eyes shut. "No, I'm not talking down to y—I don't care about what Dr. K says, if he was worth a damn we'd still be—Okay, I will. *I said, I will.* I have someone right here, actually. No, he's not one of my guys, but he owes me a favor. I'm looking at him right now.

Yup." Dan could hear the voice on the other line still talking as Jackie hung up.

"I was lying of course. You don't owe me a favor, you owe me money. So, change of plan," Jackie said. "You work for me now."

"What does that mean?" Dan said.

"Shut up and listen," he said. "My daughter is missing. Her mom is worried to death—she hasn't heard from her in weeks. Said she was hanging 'round with this one kid back in New York. The ex only met him twice. Lydia didn't bring him around all that much—blah, blah. She's not answering calls, *yadda, yadda, etcetera,* and no one knows how to get in touch with the boy she was with. She's overreacting, which makes her overbearing. Lydia likes her space, always has, I get it. You would too if you had to deal with that fucking psycho. The ex thought maybe Lydia was out here with me, but I haven't seen her in a few years."

"Almost four," Eyebrows said.

Jackie looked at him, confused and angry. "What?"

"It's been almost four years since she's been around, sir. That's all I meant."

"But now you derailed my train of thought," Jackie said. He turned to Dan. "I'm sure she's fine, but her mom will be riding my goddamn ass from now until she shows up. Last time she did this, it took these two, what, three weeks, to find her. Where was she that time?"

"Out east, I think it was," Eyebrows said. "Atlanta."

"So, what we're going—"

"Sorry," Eyebrows said. Jackie's face lost all expression. "That time it was actually just about three towns over. Atlanta was the time before that."

"...Yes. What we're go—"

"What's this got to do with me?" Dan chimed in.

Jackie's words came out in a growl. "Goddamn it! Everyone stop interrupting me!" His face red and puffy. "You. Shut up," he said, pointing at Eyebrows. He poked Dan in the chest. "And you! You're going to find her," Jackie said. "You find her, and your debt will be canceled out. You get away with your life, and you get out of mine."

"How the fuck am I supposed to do that? Get one of these assholes to do it."

Eyebrows drove his elbow into Dan's back, almost dropping him to his knees.

"These assholes work for me, Dan," he said. "Actually work. They aren't some freeloading drunken loser that owes me money. I have other things I need them to be doing, more important things."

"More important than your daughter? No wonder she hates you."

Jackie's lip twitched with frustration. He punched Dan in the face, opening his eyebrow again. The two goons caught him on the way down.

"First of all, Dan, Fuck. You. She doesn't hate me. And B, nothing is more important than my baby girl. They aren't on the job because it's bullshit. It's all bullshit. It just keeps this bitch off of my ass. I don't need them running around wasting their time, *again*, only to find her shacked up with some guy and her phone off. It'd be a waste of their time. And more importantly, mine. It's a perfect use of your time, though, isn't it?" Jackie paused. "Why am I even having this conversation? This isn't a discussion, Dan. It's the way it is. Uncuff him."

The freedom of his hands was the most glorious thing Dan had ever felt. Better than any drunk, any high, any screw he's ever had. If he could have bottled that feeling, he would have. He rubbed his wrist and saw his hand for the first time. Contorted and swollen and not the color it should be.

"Block your wife's number and wait for your daughter to come back. Two birds," Dan said.

"*This fucking guy*," Jackie said, followed by a sucker punch to the gut. Dan collapsed to his knees, no one bothering to catch him. Dan tried to look defiant as he stood up, but it came across clumsy. "Plenty more jokes where that came from? Or are you finally done?"

Dan spat blood on the ground. "I don't even know where to start. I have no idea what she even looks like."

"Pretty girl," Eyebrows said.

"What is this?" Jackie's patience gone. "What are you doing?"

"I was just—" Eyebrows started.

"I know what you were *just*, but enough with the peanut gallery horseshit—so help me God."

"Sorry Jack," Eyebrows said.

"Shut up," Jackie said. "Dan, I'll text you a picture. You have a month, kid."

A month. Dan put all his effort into hiding his smile. Jackie was as dumb as he was in high school. Super Senior. Give him a month, and Dan would be more gone than anyone had ever been gone before. Like smoke from a broken bottle. Vapor. This felt better than getting the handcuffs off. *A month, got it. I won't let you down, Jack. You can count on me.* Play it like that, then hit the road and not look back. Dan would take his head start and disappear. Fuck New Mexico anyway. He'd learn to ice fish in Maine, he'd be so far away from this place.

Windows down, the road as straight and flat as anything Dan could imagine. The horizon like the dot of an i, no, smaller than that. A speck. One that led to freedom. Fat Jackie and this shithole state behind him. *Yes sir, right away sir, anything else sir,* that's all he had to say. But Dan's mouth was always faster than his brain, and more petty—always writing a hell of a check that he had to find a way to cash with nothing but three pennies and a bottle cap in his pocket.

And Dan really hated being called kid.

The vision of him driving to freedom disappeared, and all he could see was a memory—Jackie, his second senior year, taking that bat to the headlights of Dan's car, before spider-webbing the windshield. He needed the car for work. It was a piece of shit by the time Dan even got it, a purple Dodge Neon, but he used every ounce of cash he could scrape together to buy it. The thing threw blue smoke, and the muffler scraped along the road, soda-coated pennies glued to the bottom of the cup holders. But it ran, and it was his. Dan was heading to the parking lot, backpack slung to one side, lighting a cigarette, and there was Jackie, swinging with all his might, shaking his hands after each hit. All over some girl. Or maybe it was money, Dan couldn't remember. Some people just never stop being assholes.

Dan couldn't catch his mouth.

"A month? To find one girl, between New Mexico and New York. That's fucking bullshit, man. I'm just a free-loading loser, man. Don't trust me with this shit."

"A *drunk* freeloading loser. A month, or I collect my money the same way I was about to collect it. Do you get what I'm saying?"

"Of course I do, asshole. I'm not a moron. You're about as subtle as a goddamn sledgehammer."

"A month. Get out of my sight. I'm sick of you. It's plenty of time, kid. Get."

Dan-A-Plenty, God, Dan hated that nickname and how clever Jackie thought it was. *Plenty of schemes, plenty of jokes...Yeah, and plenty of times I fingered your girlfriend under the bleachers for smashing up my car, you fat fuck.* Dan surveyed Jackie, standing there with the black smudge across his forehead in what probably resembled a cross at one point—he couldn't stop his mouth if he tried. But by this point he wasn't trying.

"How about forty days," Dan lifted his fucked-up hand, motioning to Jackie's head. "It's Ash Wednesday, seems fitting."

"There he is again, fellas, *Dan-A-Plenty.* Plenty of smart-ass remarks. Only seems right," he said, shaking his head in disbelief. "Well, asshole, now you only have two weeks."

"Jackie, two weeks? Come on, be serious. You give me two weeks to find a missing person. I'm not a detective. Okay, okay, it was a dumb joke. A month, got it."

"No, you don't *got it,* Dan," he said. "All these years later...when will you just learn to *Shut Your Fucking Mouth.* You have a week. Got any more jokes?"

"A week! You want her found, right? I need more time than that."

"She'll be found with or without you, Dan," Jackie laughed in disbelief. "You still don't understand anything. You don't matter. Get me my money or find my girl. Those are your only options. Option three is still on the table, too, if that suits you." He waved the gun.

"Okay, fuck. A week."

"Now get out of my sight."

"Can I at least get a ride—"

Jackie fired his gun in the air. Everyone jumped and tried to plug their ears, but the damage was already done. The room sounded underwater, with muffled voices and a high-pitched mosquito buzz infesting their brains. *"Get the fuck out of my goddamn face!"* Jackie screamed but Dan couldn't hear it. He could only watch the redness deepening in his face, and the large vein cutting diagonally across his forehead, raising a line through the smudged ash. Dan, finger-wiggling in his ear, kept opening his mouth and working his jaw side to side, trying to pop something loose so he could hear normally again.

"Hey Dan." Jackie's voice slogged through the underwater current of the room, muffled and low. "Your entire life only amounts to ten grand. Pretty pathetic, huh?" He and his goons shook with laughter like a silent movie, their voices beginning to take hold as the sounds of the room came back to life again—the wet grit underfoot, water oozing down the walls, and their stupid, moronic giggling.

Dan walked past them and out the door, down the narrow hallway of flickering fluorescent lights, the glass tapping every time a bulb popped on. Dan kept walking, paying no attention to the rooms that lined the hallway, only focused on the door at the end that never seemed to be getting any closer. Staying impossibly far, even as the laughter behind him got further away. Finally, the door loomed large in front of him, and he pushed the bar with his hip, his broken hand still cradled in the other. Free!

He could still get far enough away in a week if he left first thing in the morning. The door crashed shut behind him with a metal thud, and Dan stood on the dark, empty street, surrounded by abandoned warehouses, with no covering to protect him from the rain.

2

JACKIE, THAT FAT FUCK. OF COURSE HE would leave him in the middle of nowhere in the goddamn rain with a hand that was busted to shit and no money. Dan stopped walking and looked to the darkness above him, the rain falling on his face. It was cooling at first, but mostly it was the sudden realization that his phone was still back in his motel room. He was stuck. It never rained, why tonight of all nights? Aside from the pain in his hand and the sharp sting in his ribs, Dan's stomach was also killing him. He couldn't remember the last time he ate. He'd be home nursing a hangover if Jackie didn't come knocking. Part of him was glad that he wasn't lying on the bathroom floor in his underwear, soaking up the coldness from the tiles and clinging to the side of his toilet, swearing that he'd never drink again. He couldn't decide whether it was worth the gash across his eyebrow and a broken hand, though. Probably some sort of fracture in his ribs, too, the way it hurt when he breathed. Good thing he wasn't sticking around, because how the fuck was he supposed to find this girl? How does anyone find anyone? He had no resources or connections. All of it relied on Jackie coming through with a photo. And if he didn't, then Dan would have nothing at all. Less than nothing. A name? That's it—Lydia. Fuck that.

He picked a direction and started walking. He could be heading further from home for all he knew but he needed an intersection or a street name to work with, a major road. So far, nothing. Building after building of dark, empty warehouses, just rows of broken and cloudy windows. Junk yards, auto glass and repair, and endless lines of chain link fences topped with barbed wire. He walked for what felt like forever before he came to a sign that said the airport was five miles in the direction he came from. Cursing out loud to no one but the rain, Dan turned around and began walking back to his motel.

Dan's sneakers squished along the stained green carpet of his room—thin and worn out, running wall to wall, except for the parts that were ripped and showed the rotting wood underneath, more rug than a carpet. The door jamb was busted when he got back, scuffed with the boot marks from Jackie's guys. He didn't know how he was going to pay for the door and couldn't think about it right now. He was wet and tired and only had a week to live if he didn't make a run for it. Dan closed the door the best he could. He propped the dresser onto the top of his foot, and in an awkward motion, with his good hand, he lifted his leg and pulled it back, slowly and clumsily sliding the dresser across the carpet until it was pinning the door closed. He leaned on the dresser, kicked off his shoes, and pulled off his wet socks, his feet pale and pruned. He left his jeans and bloody shirt on the carpet by the dresser and stood naked in the bathroom, assessing his face and his hand and the bruising on his ribs while he waited for the water to heat up.

His hair was greasy and wet and stuck to his forehead, and the stubbled shadow of his beard was dyed red with mud and blood. The grime from the cement filled the wrinkles around his eyes, except for zebra streaks of grit alternating down his neck where the sweat and spit, and rain cleaned away the dirt.

Dan fought the urge to look away and stared himself in the eyes. They were defeated and tired now. "You're a real piece of work," he said. "What did you get yourself into this time?"

Dan made an okay living as a garbage man. Nothing fancy, but he didn't need much. He ate, he drank, and he worked. He was set up for retirement, had a pension. All he had to do was deal with his back and knees aching. He could have done that. Now here he was with Jackie standing on his neck. He didn't know shit about investing, or what the hell a Ponzi scheme even was. Once the steam collected on the mirror, covering his reflection in a haze, Dan got into the shower and hoped the heat from the water and the thick mist rising around him would help rid him of this night—of the pain, of the dirt, and of fat fucking Jackie and his two asshole thugs.

He was tired and hungry, but moving the dresser again so he could go out and eat seemed like too much effort. His phone was dead, so he had no idea if Jackie sent him any helpful information. He didn't care. Not like he needed it. His exhaustion and hunger made him wish he was already dead. Why drag it out for another week? He knew he was just exhausted and in the morning he'd feel better, and make a plan to leave town and be done with Jackie. He opened the drawer by his bed where he stashed his charger and plugged in his phone without turning it on. He took the Bible from the drawer and placed it on the bed, then grabbed an old, stained undershirt from his dresser. Using his teeth to get a small tear started, he pulled the shirt apart into makeshift straps. He laid them out on the bed, spaced as evenly as he could manage, and placed the Bible on top. Then, putting his busted hand as flat as he could, like he was getting sworn in to testify, he used his free hand and teeth to tie the strips as tightly as he could, fastening his hand to the book.

Dan lay on the bed looking up at the ceiling with its discolored paint and water stains, but he couldn't sleep. Not with the throbbing coursing through his hand and up his arm. He wished this were a smoking room. And he wished that he still smoked. All the beer bottles on the nightstand were empty. He leaned over as far as he could and felt around the ground under the bed, hoping there would be a bottle of something down there. Anything that could numb the pain and help him sleep. But all he could find was the remote. Out of the corner of his eye, a bone dry plastic jug of cheap whiskey sat on the floor, mocking him. That was the closest he'd have to any relief, teased by empties. The TV was about thirty years old, square, and made of glass and tubes. Only a handful of channels came in cleanly, so he settled on the quietest one he could find, for background noise. The Twilight Zone. Dan had seen this episode before—a man with a strange voice selling trinkets on the front steps of an apartment building, making a big pitch about his toys, with another man in a dark suit entering the scene. Dan fell asleep during the commercial break.

Dan woke himself with a sharp snore that hurt his face, and the jump scare brought all the pain that was still sleeping in him to life—passing through his blood like oxygen. The light in the room made him want to vomit, and he could already feel the dryness in his mouth and the post-nasal drip from walking in the rain. Now he could add feeling like shit to the feeling of death he had before he fell asleep. His hand hurt worse than it did last night, and now it was various shades of green and dark purple. He couldn't tell if his homemade splint made any difference, but he untied the strips of ripped shirt and tried to see what he could bend. Only his pinky and ring finger moved, the top of his middle finger curling slightly. He ended up paying for that experiment as the motions awoke every nerve ending and receptor in his arm and shot them all up through his brain like bolts of lightning. *I need to get something for this pain.* Maybe he could get his hand put into a cast, but he needed to hit the road in a hurry, so it didn't feel worth it.

Dan sat on the edge of the bed and rubbed his feet on the carpet, hoping for some comfort, but it was only a small step up from dragging his feet across wood. He turned his phone on and walked into the bathroom while it booted up. The tile was cold, and he sloshed over his wet towel on the floor. He flinched when he saw all the blood on his face, the cut over his eye opening in his sleep. Peeking his head out of the bathroom door, he saw his pillow, now two-toned, half white and half maroon. He ran the water and looked through the cabinet for a bandage, only finding an old, off-white colored band-aid stuck in the crease of one of the drawers. He dug it out and opened the mirror to see if there was any Tylenol. Only a bottle of ibuprofen. He didn't check the expiration date, just poured a few into his mouth and started chewing.

The water was running, but still cold, and Dan's impatience got the best of him. He cupped the water into his hands and splashed some on his face. The coldness of it sent a sharp ache down the bones of his hand, a throb that hurt to the core, as if the marrow itself was trying to break out. He rubbed the cut along his eyebrow, watching the water turn red. He didn't have a clean towel, so he picked the one from the floor, turning it in his hands until he found a dry area before patting his face. It took more pressure than he'd like to have used on his tender brow, but he finally got the band-aid to stick. His phone beeped from the other room—chirp after chirp, the vibrations steadily buzzing throughout each alert.

Ten new messages, all texts, no calls, and all of them from Fat Jackie. The first photo was of a girl, maybe in her early twenties. She had two rings in her nose and three in each ear. Her hair was multicolored, black and red and purple, and she had a ring through her septum. Her neck, chest, and throat were tattooed solid black, no design, no pattern, just black ink. The darkness wrapped around the corners of her face, thinly around the jaw, narrowing to a point below her ear. Six dots were tattooed over one of her eyebrows, evenly spaced out and tapering down smaller. A series of thin lines were tattooed across her ears and onto the side of her head, continually, like scratches. That was all that could be seen in the photo, which was just a picture taken of a computer screen. The rest of the messages were screen captures of social media profiles—Dan's mother, his sister, an uncle he didn't talk to anymore, a cousin, and some old high school friends—a text message followed that said: *If you run, your debt is on their heads. One week.*

Well, shit.

Running was the only thing Dan considered. Getting back to the motel, grabbing some of his shit—not all of it, just enough—maybe boost the TV for some extra cash if it wasn't bolted down, and taking off. Head into Mexico, or maybe up north somewhere, maybe Montana. Learn how to fly fish, find a job at a gas station, become a park ranger, or something small-town and wholesome. Maybe they'd have a casino. There were a lot of reservations up there, at least he thought there were. He could deal Blackjack or man the Craps table.

But he never thought about his mom or sister, or how they could have been brought into this. They would have fallen for it, too, any sort of schmoozing that Fat Jackie would pour onto them. Maybe spinning some shit about having a crush on his sister back in high school, flexing his wealth like a lure. Mom always did like Jackie. He knew how to charm and disarm when he needed to. They'd welcome him right in, probably offer him homemade crumb cake or ask him to stay for dinner, never knowing they were sharing a meal with the devil. Their kindness wouldn't do anything for him either. He wouldn't soften. He'd turn on them and do it with joy. Shit, he might kill Dan and still do them just because that was the type of asshole he was. A real piece of shit. Always has been. Always will be.

Dan wasn't sure if Jackie would act on this impulse, but in a weird way, he thought he should thank him for this flash of enlightenment, even though it filled Dan with a searing rage. He felt he could have crushed the phone in his hand, he was so angry. Instead, he threw the TV remote at the wall, the back exploded, and the batteries popped out, clanging and rolling on the floor. He took a deep breath and focused back on the photo of Lydia. Maybe there was some hope in that she was so distinctive. The tiniest chance that if someone came across her they would remember.

But deep in his gut he knew, and the realization ached worse than his hand—

Dan knew he was fucked.

He knew all he was doing was treading water until he eventually drowned. He looked at the photo and the girl's haunting eyes. Focusing on her face until the tattoos and piercings blurred and disappeared from his mind, trying to find something in those eyes to cling to, something to make him care and find hope that he could pull this off. Anything. But all he felt was hungry.

Dan hung his head, defeated before trying. He checked his wallet, which he kept in the underwear drawer of the dresser, and found it only held forty two dollars. Barely enough for some beer and breakfast at the diner. Maybe Annie would be working. That would be a good sign. A ray of hope that not everything was fucked. If she was working, he'd get through this. He'd survive and find the girl, and everything would be okay.

Dan dug his feet into the floor and used his hips to move the dresser enough to squeeze out the door. He'd have to come up with a better fix soon, but right now he needed a drink. A drink and something to eat. A drink and something to eat, and possibly a pack of cigarettes. Maybe he'll pick up smoking again, no reason not to. He walked to his car only to realize he left his keys on the table by the bed. He didn't feel like squeezing through the door again and back out, so he began walking to the diner.

3

IT WASN'T EVEN NOON, AND THE AIR WAS already hot and oppressive. Dan was dehydrated from the night before and the night before that. Maybe walking was a bad idea. The passing cars threw dirt in the air that floated weightlessly in the draft between the automobiles before getting tossed in Dan's face. He shielded his eyes from the dust, already in a permanent half-squint from the sun, holding his breath as he passed through each cloud. He saw the heat rising from the ground in the distance—the road rippling like a lake in front of the gas station. Dan's throat was so dry. Everything sucked. What was he supposed to do when he found this girl anyway? Convince her to come home? Was he just supposed to locate where she was and tell Fat Jackie? That was it? He couldn't imagine it being that simple. Nothing in his life was ever simple, especially when Jackie was involved.

The gas station was quiet and empty, the last car in the parking lot driving off as Dan walked up. The store was cool, and the hum of the A/C came to life when he opened the door, the cold air falling over him like an avalanche. It felt amazing. He wished he could sit in there all day, but the low temperature put a deep ache in the bones of his busted hand. The woman working behind the counter was heavyset, and her hair wasn't its natural color, such a deep black it was almost blue, but the roots by her scalp were showing brown. She had a tribal tattoo that looked like ivy inked on the inside of her ear, and another of a heart with a banner and a name that Dan couldn't see tattooed on the front of her chest. She looked up when Dan entered and the door chimed, but went back to her phone. Even after he gave a polite smile and nod, she only glanced at him then back down without acknowledging any of his gestures.

His body was telling him to buy a Gatorade, or a coconut water, anything to hydrate him—the desert air ringing all the moisture from him, leaving only a tongue that stuck to his mouth and some crusty blood lining his nose. But instead, he grabbed a tall boy of Bud Light and put it on the counter. He thought of picking up something to eat, to hold him over until he got to the diner, maybe some beef jerky, but money was tight, and he'd rather have a bigger breakfast and not risk being light on a tip for Annie.

The girl lifted her eyes from her phone, looked him up and down, then side-eyed his beer. "I can't sell you that," she said.

"I'm flattered, I'll show you I.D."

"That's well and good, but I still can't sell it to you." She pointed over her shoulder to the clock on the wall, never looking up from her screen. "Too early."

"Oh, give me a break. I had a terrible night, and my fucking hand is killing me, just sell me the goddamn beer."

"Cussing ain't gonna get you the beer, so you can stop wit' all that. Come back later 'n you can buy all the beer you can carry."

Dan pulled out his phone and opened the picture of Lydia. "Do you know this girl?"

She studied the picture with more attention than Dan was expecting. "Should I?"

"I suppose not. It was a long shot. Thanks."

"No problem. Can I do anything else for you today, sir? Maybe some gas or a newspaper?" Dan looked at the stack of newspapers in front of the counter, still zipped into neat stacks. The headline was bold and red, some cheesy pun about a stockbroker murdered in New York days ago, BULL TOO MUCH TO BEAR. STOCK PLUMMETS ON NYPD AS KILLER STILL AT LARGE. "Maybe try one of our new breakfast taquitos?" Her voice was unenthused, as if she was reading from a script.

"Nope, just the beer."

"I already told y—"

"Oh fuck this," Dan said, and took a five-dollar bill out of his wallet, which was more than the beer cost, put it on the counter, and grabbed the can. "Keep the change," he said, walking out the door. As he left, he heard a commotion behind him, but she never followed after. The pop, crack, and sizzle of the carbonation when he opened the can made Dan's mouth water and sent a shock of excitement through his body. The coldness of the first sip felt like the tongue of an angel kissing him and slithering down his throat. Nothing ever tasted so good. He was surprised that he was already feeling something, but he was guzzling, and it was hot, and he had nothing in his stomach. Maybe it was all in his head, but it made his hand hurt less, so he was happy about that.

In hindsight, he figured he should have bought some sort of aspirin at the gas station, but he couldn't go back now. He needed the money for breakfast, anyway. He really hoped Annie was working.

The diner was old-timey or at least meant to look that way. It was long and thin, and the outside was modeled to look like a train car. The inside only had a few tables and booths, the rest was counter seating. Everything was stainless steel and red vinyl. There were no TVs, just jukeboxes in each booth, and an oldies station that played through speakers built into the ceiling. Their breakfast was no frills, and that's what Dan liked about it the most. Cheap and greasy. A mist sprayed across the doorway that coated Dan's skin in a refreshing dew, and then the cool air from the A/C hit, and it was better than lemonade on a hot day, better than jumping into a swimming pool. Cold air had a smell to it. Dan couldn't place it, but refrigerators and freezers smelled of it, and the diner did too. Annie was finishing ringing up a customer when Dan walked in. Her face lit up when she saw him, but he could tell she tried to stifle it. It was the best part of any day—that flash of unbridled excitement before she quickly squashed it down.

Annie was short. Not laughably short. Maybe petite would be the right word—she came up to Dan's nose. Dan didn't usually go for blondes, but Annie dyed her hair more of a grey color and, man, did it do something for him. He always flirted with her, but he never pulled the trigger. She'd always flirt back, and whenever he thought he crossed the line, she'd respond before he could even gear up for an apology, and the line would move that much further along. He didn't know why the ring on her finger was stopping him or even causing him to hesitate. Maybe it was more respect for her than for the gold band and whoever was on the other side of it.

She looked concerned when she saw the state he was in, and that was before she noticed his hand. He shot her a wink, as casually as he could, to reassure her. It might have worked, he thought, because she smiled that crooked smile and nodded toward the empty booth in the back. When he sat down, he grabbed the menu, which was only one page, laminated front and back. He flipped it over a few times absent-mindedly, already knowing what he was going to get. The same thing he always got—runny eggs to mix into some well-done hash browns, rye toast, bacon, and coffee with a drop of half and half.

A chubby waitress came over, plump and nice, really milking the dimples in her cheeks and the way the top of her breasts ballooned from of her collar. She was cheery and flipped to an empty page of her pad. When Dan politely told her he was waiting for Annie, the woman shrugged, never losing her cheerfulness, and walked to the counter to swap places with her.

Usually when she came over, Annie would put on an old-school waitress vibe, the kind that said cliché shit like *'What can I get fir ya, pal? The usual?'* and had the pad flip open and shut quickly like a police officer writing a ticket, putting her weight on one hip, leaning off to the side, chewing invisible gum. But today she walked over in a rush, concern painting her face, a gentleness to her smile.

"Oh my God, Dan, what happened?" She spoke fast and loud enough that it made him self-conscious.

He waved his good hand in front of his face as if he was brushing the trouble out of the air between them. "Long story."

"Are you okay?"

"I'm not sure. I'll know soon enough."

"Let me get you your food," she said, and turned to leave. He grabbed her hand.

"A Bloody Mary, too," he said, instead of his usual coffee. "I don't need anything fancy in it, just celery."

"Oh hun," she said, gently cupping his chin and lifting his head toward the light. "You're bleeding."

"I thought I got it to stop." He felt around the loose band-aid, half attached, half flapping in the breeze. He reached for some napkins and pressed them to his face.

"Go into the restroom and wait for me," she said. "Let me go grab our first aid." Dan liked his chin resting in her hand, forcing them to make uninterrupted eye contact. His gaze flowed from her eyes to her mouth, down her neck, over the front of her chest, and along her slender arm. He could have sworn that she rubbed his face as she let go of his chin. She was still wearing her soft smile when she walked away.

The bathroom was all metal. Metal walls, metal stalls, a metal sink. It was shiny and bright and cold and sterile. He looked at himself in the mirror, removing the band-aid, folding it in half, and placing it on the sink. The cut was bad, he knew he needed stitches, but what did he care about a scar anymore? When Jackie was through with him, they'd probably have a closed casket anyway, if they ever found his body. He washed the blood from his hands and dried them on the back of his jeans, then went over to the urinal to try and go before Annie got there. His piss was bright yellow like a highlighter and acidic, reeking of dehydration.

He finished up and was rewashing his hands when Annie walked in. She looked different. It felt like when he was a kid and saw a teacher out of school, at the store, or the movies. There was something unnatural about it. She wasn't wearing her apron, but there was more to it than that, but he couldn't put his finger on it. He thought about being alone with Annie often, one-on-one, usually in a car or back at his place. Never in the bathroom of her job. It wasn't ideal, but it did stir an excitement in his stomach, and he had to breathe deep and calm himself as the idea alone made his blood rush downward. When she turned and latched the door, his face tingled, and sweat percolated along his hairline.

"Okay, let me take a look at this." She placed the first aid kit on the counter. "Here," she said, and handed him some paper towels, "you better wash that before we start messing around." She opened both sides of the faucet, running her slender fingertips through the water, waiting for it to heat up. Dan cupped his hands and splashed it over his face, watery blood leaking down his temple and cheek. He soaped up his hands, running them over the cut, and rinsed again. Instead of giving him the paper towel, Annie gently dabbed the wound herself and dried around it, then pressed the paper to it and reached for his bad hand. He winced when she grabbed it and placed it gently over the paper towel.

"So, what's this long story?"

Dan thought about whether he should tell her the truth or gloss over it. This all felt so intimate that he wasn't sure he could have lied to her if he wanted to. "It's—well, no, it's actually a pretty short story. I had money, lost it. A guy loaned me more money, and I lost that. I tried to borrow more to pay *that* back, then lost it too. Horses, before you ask. The last time, anyway. The first loss was a bad stock market...thing. It's not that much money, to him at least—ten grand. But we've had it out for each other since high school." He leaned back on the sink, the slouching putting the two of them at eye level. "There's history."

"So, he did this to you?"

"Yeah, him and his two stupid guys. And—"

Annie sat next to him on the sink with the first aid kit on her lap and was sorting through the compartments of bandages, waiting. She turned to face him, holding up a thin butterfly bandage.

"They have these for the cooks. It'll hold better." She rubbed a yellow liquid from the case over the cut in his eye and applied the bandage. "And?" she said. "His two stupid guys, and?"

"He gave me a week to find his missing daughter, which pays off my debt. Or..."

"Or?"

Dan just gave her a look.

"Oh," she said. The corner of her mouth bunched with unease. "You think he would? If it came down to it?"

"Yeah. He almost did last night."

"But he didn't, so—"

"Because he got a phone call about his daughter before he could."

"I see," she said and grabbed his bad hand. "Okay, let's find her." It was the way she said *let's*—let's find her. Dan didn't know if she meant it or if it slipped out. Annie held his hand in hers, small and slender, thin fingers and a tiny wrist that made her bracelets look oversized. She moved her fingers back and forth over his hand. "There's nothing I can do about this though, I'm afraid."

"That's what the Bloody Mary is for. Do you have any painkillers in there?"

"Aspirin only, nothing strong."

"I'll take it," he said.

Annie opened a package in his hand, and he asked for another one. He chewed the pills, and she turned on the faucet again before stepping back so Dan could drink from it. He wiped his face with the back of his hand, and the two locked eyes for a moment. He felt a strong desire to close the space between them—a desire he couldn't fight, not that he tried. He felt so close to her right now, like something from a dream. Without thinking, he found his hand was back in hers. He leaned in slowly, and she didn't move away. As he got as near as possible before actually kissing, she shifted her face to the side, avoiding his advance. She rested her forehead on his, and they stayed there without exchanging words. No apologies.

They stood together, hand in hand.

She cleared her throat softly, the echo rolling loudly through the still room, bouncing off the steel. "Do you have a picture of the girl?"

He sat up and dug his phone out of his pocket, Annie never letting go of his other hand. He showed her the picture.

"Oh hey! I know her!"

Dan's eyes lit up.

"Sorry, that wasn't funny. I didn't know what I was— Here, let me take a better look." She took the phone, the embarrassment from the failed joke painted on her face. "She's pretty. Really pretty."

"You think? I think she looks kind of weird."

"Be nice. She might not be your style, but she's so pretty."

Dan shrugged his shoulders. "Well, the good news is, she's anywhere between here and"—he pretended to do calculations in his head, mumbling under his breath, his eyes rolled up to the ceiling in thought, *and carry the one.* He stopped and grinned. "Between here and New York. That's the last place anyone saw her. At least according to her mom." He gave a defeated laugh that came out as a short burst of air. "It's impossible. I mean, that's why he's having me do it, right? A fuck-up on a task where fucking-up is the only outcome. No success, just the illusion. A carrot on a stick. God, he's *such* an asshole."

Annie sat back next to him on the sink. "Don't say that, you're not a fuck-up."

Dan looked over at her. "I am, though. I appreciate it, but—"

"Hmm, I disagree, but there's time for that later. Right now, we have this, and we're not defeated yet. We can do it." She closed the first aid kit. "We just gotta think." Her voice lowered to a whisper, and she took her hand from his for the first time. She looked at him with her face scrunched, chewing on the inside corner of her lip. "Know what I'm thinking? I don't know if it's anything, though."

"It's more than I got."

"She kind of looks, like, I dunno, punky, maybe. Is that a word? Punky? Like, kind of like a rocker chick. With the whole, you know, face tattoos and all that black. So maybe we can go to that venue downtown, the one by the used car place. Not the one with the billboard, but the one with that big sign, the digital one. I mean, maybe someone there might know her, right?"

Dan was full of optimism for the first time. "No, that's great! That's something! More than I thought I'd have."

"Really? You set a low bar, huh?"

"For pulling this off? Yeah, real low. You'd have to dig to reach it. But this is perfect!" He could have kissed her. A big Bugs Bunny kiss right on the mouth, with a cartoonish *mmmuuuaah*. He wanted to jump on the sink and pump his fist. He felt alive, felt hope.

"Great, I get off at eight."

"What's that?"

"I get off at eight, we'll go then."

"You already did enough, you don't need to—"

"Don't be ridiculous. Just let me go home and shower, and I'll meet you back here around nine."

"You're sure?"

"It could be fun," she said. "Well, besides the whole you know," she ran a finger across her throat with a grimace."

"Thank you," he said. "For everything."

"Let me get you that Bloody Mary."

"I almost forgot. I'm hungry as shit."

"I'll get your food too." And she left.

Dan leaned on the sink, wincing when he accidentally put weight on his hand. We. She said that a lot. We and us. He didn't feel the need to ask about her man. He didn't care. Was she really on board? Maybe it was pity. But maybe it was something else, something more. Hell, he thought, if this was his last week above ground, then pity suited him just fine.

The effects of the Bloody Mary and the tall boy were making him feel almost pain-free, and the grease from breakfast helped settle his stomach. The walk home took its toll—the heat made him sweat out more booze than he would have liked, and the airy feeling in his head started to level out, bringing back the throbbing in his hand. He found another gas station on the way back to the motel, after seeing the same lady behind the counter of the other. He spent the last of his money on two more tall boys and three packs of travel Tylenol.

4

DAN WALKED INTO THE DOOR OF HIS motel room, forgetting that he had the dresser jammed up tight against it. It was almost comical now that he was back to feeling halfway drunk, to think of himself just walking into the door with a thud like that. He didn't know if he apologized out loud or if he just said excuse me in his head. The room was a mess, still in shambles from yesterday. Dan had hours to kill before he and Annie went to the venue to see what they could find out. He didn't feel like cleaning and wanted to sit around and enjoy the remainder of his drunk, but decided to straighten up. Nothing crazy, just getting rid of the bottles and trash, picking up the towels and clothes. He did his best to fix the remote he threw, using rubber bands to hold the batteries in place.

He had no money and figured he should either try and get to an ATM or maybe he could find some stuff to sell real quick. Anything to have a few bucks to his name so that he didn't roll up to the club broke and embarrassed, needing to borrow money for drinks, or for a cover charge.

Dan gathered up the beer and liquor bottles in the room and put them in one of the clear garbage bags that lined the bottom of the can in his room. He was able to get the door open enough without having to move the dresser to get an arm out and drop the bag outside. He gathered his clothes and towels and put them in another bag, and tossed that outside as well. That did a lot to clean the room. He made the bed and used a t-shirt to cover his blood-stained pillow. He threw away his plates and Chinese food containers along with napkins and receipts, and some bible tracts left on his windshield. He made sure he had his keys this time and moved the dresser just enough to squeeze his body through, and reaching his arm back inside, he grabbed what he could and inched the dresser until the door was mostly shut. He threw the bags of bottles and clothes in the back seat of his car and the garbage into the dumpster. He surveyed the contents of his trunk—a spare donut, a tire iron, and a car jack, towels, some stained with oil and grease, and a pair of jumper cables that could jump a battery without another car. He moved them to the back seat along with the tire iron and car jack and left on his quest to make a few bucks for the night.

The only two working bottle machines were on opposite sides of the little vestibule, and Dan separated the bottles into glass and plastic and ran each through their machines, collecting the few dollars it spat out in return. Not much, but it would be enough to do his laundry. The laundromat was a few blocks from the supermarket, and from there it was a quick drive to Pudgie's. He dumped all the clothes into one machine, not bothering to separate them since he didn't have the money for more than the one load anyway. He set the machine to heavy duty and let it run. The timer said he had about forty minutes.

Pudgie's shop, or *Shoppe* as his sign said, was a typical pawn shop with the windows caged up in tight, small links, covered in rust and grime. The sign looked like it could have been high-end and fashionable at one time, but Pudgie never updated, and now the neon Open sign was chipped with some of the letters not glowing at all. But Pudgie was the closest, and he gave a good price, which was all Dan really cared about. He took Dan's high school ring a few months back and gave him over five hundred dollars for it. Gave him eight hundred for his grandfather's watches—an old pocket watch given to him by Dan's grandmother, back from when she and his pop-pop were just dating, and a fancy gold watch he got from his platoon when they got home from the war. All Dan knew was that his grandfather did something brave and saved just about the whole lot of them, and the watch was their gift for it—he never learned the whole story, and his pop-pop never wanted to talk about it.

Dan regretted selling it, but times were rough, and he was out a place to stay, with only his car to his name, and no money for booze. *Any port in a storm*, he justified to himself, to feel better about it. But the next time he was in there, hocking a waffle iron he found at a garage sale, along with some of his dad's old fishing lures, he saw that the watch was already gone. It sucked, but the appliance got him enough to drink himself to sleep over it. Pudgie always did give a good price.

"Hey Pudge," Dan said, the buzzer stopping when the door closed behind him, tire iron under his arm and jack in his hand, the jumper cables balanced on top.

"Daniel, my friend! What happened to you?" Dan couldn't place his accent. Maybe Africa. But not lion Africa, camel Africa, some place people didn't realize was Africa, where they probably wore fezzes and bells rung at certain times of day. At least that's what Dan pictured in his head whenever Pudgie greeted him like that. He had the cleanest teeth Dan had ever seen, shining brightly against his olive skin, except for one dead tooth. Brown and dull in the middle of all of that pure white. "What can I do for you today? What have you brought for me?"

Dan dumped everything on the glass counter by the register that held all the rings and watches. "How much for all of this? "

Pudgie looked over the contents and scratched the stubble on his chin. "My friend, this tire iron, maybe I give you ten, make it, say, twelve dollars. For this, to jack up car, it's nice, looks new, hydraulic, yes? I'll give you fifty for it. And this machine, to jump car, I give you sixty for. How much is that, I said?"

"A hundred and twenty-two dollars."

"My friend, for you, I'll round it all up. One hundred and twenty-five dollars to you. You take this deal?"

"Yeah, I'll take it."

"Very good, very good." As Pudge punched the keys of his old cash register, Dan placed his phone on the glass display case.

"Have you seen this girl by any chance?"

"She looks like a wild girl, this one, no? Is that real tattoo on her face?"

"I believe so."

"Sorry, my friend, I don't see her. Maybe you talk to the man who does that to her. Pretty girl, real shame."

"Thanks anyway." Dan took his money and left. He headed back to the laundromat, first stopping off at a gas station to make sure he had enough in his tank for the night. He also bought two tall boys of Bud and drank them out of a paper bag while he watched his clothes tumble in the dryer. He searched on his phone for tattoo shops in the area and took note. He had gotten another jolt of excitement when Pudge mentioned the idea. He didn't know if he would have thought about that. Maybe Annie would have, she probably already did, who knows. But, as he watched his shirts and pants tumble over each other like the beer swirling around in his stomach, pumping clouds into his brain, he felt that maybe he wasn't doomed, maybe he could scratch out a miracle. Snatch victory from the jaws of defeat. It was only a puncher's chance, but now he had two leads on where to start, and that was a lot better than he had before.

Dan had nothing to do after the laundromat except wait for Annie to be done with work. Back in his motel room, he wanted to fix the door, but was feeling too lazy from the beer and went to sleep for a bit. He woke with plenty of time to shower and brush his teeth. Annie was married, but he still didn't want to risk smelling like all he'd been doing was drinking and sitting in his sweat all day, waiting for her. His head was killing him, so he chewed three aspirin and washed them down with water from the shower head. He tried to lean forward, bracing himself to let the water wash over him and down his back, but the coolness of the tile sent a deep ache through his hand, and he hoped the aspirin would kick in soon. But then again, he didn't know how pain medicine worked.

When he pulled up to the diner, Annie was already waiting for him. She was leaning against the building, her hair up in a messy bun that looked like something out of a magazine, still wet from a shower. Dan's head was feeling better, but still light, and the scent of his newly washed shirt amplified the tingling that trickled through his body. She hopped into the passenger side and gave him a hug, which caught him off guard. Aside from helping him bandage his face, they've been scarce on any physical contact. If anything, just some occasional stolen grazes of their hands, a lingering touch here and there, unless he imagined all of that. Her cheek pressed against his, and he thought for a moment there was a hidden kiss, but that too was probably all in his head.

The venue was small and felt smaller because they kept a line, even though there was hardly anyone inside. An airbrushed logo was painted on the awning above the door—a grey hand covered in black fur holding up three fingers. The hand was cut off at the wrist and had a bone popping out from the bottom, blood spelling the words *The Monkey's Paw*. No one seemed to care that people were smoking inside, and after a quick look around and asking Dan if he thought it was okay, Annie screwed a cigarette into her lips and lit it. She offered it to Dan, and he was inclined to turn it down—quitting smoking was something he was proud of, and he counted the months and years like reformed alcoholics counted being dry. But when Jackie puts a bullet through his stupid fucking face next week, he doubted he'd care about that pride anymore. Plus, the way her face looked, with the lights moving over the sparse crowd, and her slim fingers holding out the cigarette towards him, filter stained with her lipstick—it was the only thing in the world he cared about.

Here's to thirty-seven months, he paused before taking it. It felt like the first time he ever smoked. The smoke crawled down his throat, slithering through the branches of his lungs, the roots spreading, mapping his insides. He couldn't remember the last time he got laid, but he knew this was better. Part of him wished he had saved it for the minutes right before Jackie pulled the trigger—to die in this moment, with this feeling, it would feel like he made it to Heaven while the Devil was still out looking for him. He closed his eyes to soak it all in, to try and burn the image of Annie's face there. Her lipstick tasted like lipstick. He didn't know why he thought it would have tasted sweet like fruit, but it still moved his stomach in loops and knots as if it did. He felt a cough climbing up his body, and choked it back until he could shrink it to the size of a grumble that he could pass off as clearing his throat. She smoked Parliaments, and he moved his thumb over the stiff filter.

Annie leaned in close and shouted into his ear so she could be heard over the music—a local band, he figured, although this type of rock music wasn't his favorite, and for all he knew, it could have been the most famous band in the country.

"I'm so relieved to be out," she said. "I haven't gone out like this in forever." Her breath was hot and light and smelled like cigarettes and white Lifesavers.

On the short drive over from the diner, the silence was awkward and thick at first—he asked how her shift was, and she wondered what he did with the rest of the day and how he was feeling. He could tell she was choosing her words carefully, probably trying to avoid mentioning her husband or any use of the words *they, we, us.* He noted it but didn't know what he was expecting. She was probably just being polite, but at the same time, he figured, maybe if she wanted to keep him at a distance, she'd be talking about her husband more. That could be something. More than anything, he was just glad the conversation flowed more easily now.

"I don't go out much either," Dan said. "Usually, I end up getting into trouble when I'm out. Or losing money."

"Or both," they said together, laughing at their overlap.

"Going out always feels like losing money to me," she said. "Especially if you're not enjoying yourself." She took a drag off her cigarette and mumbled something that sounded like *or who you're with,* but Dan wasn't sure if that last part was just what he wished he heard. "This is good, I need some excitement in my life! Adventure!"

"Freedom."

"Freedom, *yesss,*" she emphasized.

"I'm dead this time next week," he said, trying to add a joking tone to his voice. "And you never go out, so let's do this right!"

Annie looked downhearted. Then smiled. "Drinks?"

"Fucking drinks!" he said, grabbing her by the shoulders with a big grin on his face.

The bartender was bald and covered in tattoos. He must have been new and hired for his looks rather than his knowledge or experience, because when Annie asked for an Amaretto Sour, Dan could see him doing his best to look confident. Dan watched as he opened a small book behind the counter and flipped through the pages.

"Do you have any pineapple vodka?"

The bartender looked at Dan, confused. "I don't think so."

"I'll just have a whiskey, then," Dan said.

"How many fingers?"

"Fingers? You kidding?" Dan laughed. "Do I look like a fingers guy? I don't care, just pour some in a glass." The whole exchange had Dan feeling like an asshole, especially seeing the embarrassed look on the kid's face. It's not the impression he wanted to make with Annie their first time out. She had her back leaning on the bar, focused on the band, and Dan hoped she didn't hear their exchange. "Never mind, just get me a Boilermaker, thanks."

Dan didn't usually go for those hipster-type beers, but when he saw the bartender crack open a PBR, he just let it go, the setting felt right. They sat at the bar and tried to talk over the music, but stopped trying after they both got frustrated having to repeat themselves at the top of their lungs. Annie asked for another drink and put her hand on Dan's. The softness of her skin on the back of his hand was a stark contrast to the gritty, dirty stickiness of the bar top under his fingers.

In between bands the radio kicked on, and everyone

left the floor where they had been standing and jumping, and crashing into each other. The spotlights circled and zig-zagged across the room, putting on a haphazard light show for the random songs playing from the speaker. Dan looked around for a DJ but didn't see one. There were no advertisements, so Dan assumed maybe it was someone's phone on shuffle somewhere.

A Springsteen song came on, upbeat with a haze of sadness, the voice gruff and tired.

"Oh my God, I love this song," Annie said, sucking quickly on the thin mixing straw. She leaned over to Dan. "This song slaps!"

"What?"

"It slaps!"

"I don't know what that means."

"It's just something kids say when good songs come on in the diner, I don't know either." She took the straw from the glass and drank down the rest of it in two swallows. Chewing on an ice cube, her cold breath hitting his ear and falling down his neck when she leaned in and said, "Come dance with me!" She took him by the hands and dragged him onto the empty floor.

Dan resisted.

"You only have a week to live. Do you want to die not having danced one last time?"

It was the first time she ever joked about him dying. She was drunk and blunt about it, and the thought should have mixed him with some sort of grief or anxiety, but instead it lit a fire in him. He chugged the remainder of his drink and slammed it down on the bar, the shot glass clinking around inside the bigger one. Rather than resisting her pull, he ran out to the center of the floor with such enthusiasm that he got there first. Dan loved that no one else was dancing with them. When the lights passed over the darker sides of the room, he saw people laughing, some pointing, but it made him smile even more. He couldn't dance for shit, and he was happy to make a fool of himself in front of Annie. And everyone else. Drunk and not caring.

Because fuck it.

Annie danced very well, though, light on her toes, shifting her weight back and forth, ankles turning and heels coming up, bouncing on the balls of her feet, snapping her fingers. She was grinning and Dan felt a cramping in his face, laughing like a kid—he couldn't remember the last time he smiled so much it hurt. Shaking his head back and forth, his sweat caught the lights in a spray as they illuminated the dance floor, before moving on to the walls, circling over the rest of the room. His head was spinning, and his chest burned, and if he coughed, he might throw up. His mouth tasted like copper, saliva like pennies. When the light hit Annie, it cast a glow around her, a neon outline as she shifted and bounced and changed shapes. Mist spraying around her, hair melted to her face in messy wet curls.

The song stopped, and Dan imagined people would be clapping or joining in. But the music simply faded into the next one, and they were alone in the middle of the room with people laughing at them. She put her hands on his shoulders, giggling and out of breath. She tried to talk but couldn't find the air. Dan wanted to tell her he couldn't remember the last time he danced or had this much fun, hell, he couldn't remember the last time he smiled, even. But before he could, their lips were together—his good hand on her face, half-waiting for her to come to her senses and push him away. Her hand reached up and embraced his cheek. She kept kissing him. He felt her lean into him and get closer. Her lips opened more. Annie's tongue flicked against his teeth before intertwining with his.

The next band started to take the stage, the mic humming some feedback as it was set up, the hiss and pop of guitars getting plugged in, and the drummer smacking out three loud twaps on the snare drum. She stopped kissing him. Dan opened his eyes, hoping there wouldn't be a slap. An apology was forming in his head.

She leaned in over his shoulder, and into his ear she said, "Take me home."

It was the way she said *home*. He knew she didn't mean back to her house or the diner. Dan was in no condition to drive, neither was Annie, but he drove all the same for fear of losing the moment. He went slow with constant corrections to the wheel. His major concern was getting to the motel before she changed her mind. But the way her hand was working his leg, occasionally rubbing against the hardening tightness of his jeans, made him worry less. They both shared one of her cigarettes, smoke streaming from the cracked-open windows. They were at a red light, stopped more in the intersection than he realized. They looked at each other and she winked as she slowly let the smoke leak from her mouth and crawl up her face, into her nostrils, then out of her mouth again. She was sexy as hell when she did that trick, and she knew it. The blood pumped in his jeans, and he hated that he liked her so much. Usually, the type of girls Dan picked up were barflies, queens of their local dive, and he'd not care, he'd reach over, grab her head, and push it to his lap. Annie wasn't like that, though. He'd never. Dan absent-mindedly stroked himself through his jeans in a drunken haze. His mind drifted as he waited for the light to change, streetlights blurry with starbursts, the stiff outline bulging down his pant leg. She noticed what he was doing and took over, caressing him over his pants. He stopped waiting for the light to turn green and drove through the intersection and back to the motel. The car came to a crooked stop between the lines outside his door, and he scuffed his bumper on the curb.

He put the car in park, leaned over to the passenger seat, and kissed Annie, his tongue exploring her mouth and his hand her body, falling over those breasts that defied her age, nipples poking through the fabric. His mouth worked her neck, and his hand dropped down her body and pressed between her legs, feeling the warmth through her jeans. He felt her subtly grinding against his hand as she fumbled to find his button, unzipping them. He felt her slide under his waistband, her fingertips passing through the coarse hair, grazing the base of him.

"Take me inside," she said. "Now."

Dan gave her one last kiss and did his best to adjust himself enough to walk freely. He accidentally left the headlights pouring through the curtains of the room next to his. He wanted to open her door for her, but she was already outside the car and following him to his room. The door opened about a foot, then stopped with a thud. Dan cursed under his breath, pushed, then squeezed himself through the opening.

"Jackie's goons," he said, then disappeared inside. He moved the dresser away and pulled her inside. She leaned into him, and the two fell back onto the dresser. They knocked a lamp onto the floor, popping with a spark before the room went dark. They fumbled around until Dan found the TV and put it on. A blue light filled the dark spaces of the room and fell over Annie, already on the bed. Her shirt was off, and the light from the television cast shadows that danced over her in different colors. Her breasts caught the glow, gorgeous and inviting.

A white light filled the room and faded again. A reporter on the TV was talking about a Wall Street investor found dead days ago.

"This story is everywhere," Dan said, reaching behind him and turning the volume off. He crossed to the bed. He wished he could have prolonged the moment and soaked it all in, but the booze in his head and blood pumping through his body took over, and he was on her. They started to devour each other. Her breast in his mouth, and a handful of hair tugging her head back. His bad hand worked its way down under her pants and was throbbing with the pressure created from the tight space. She was warm and wet, and he felt like he was in high school again as his fingers explored the depths of her body. He kissed her neck and pinched her nipple between his teeth. She moved her hips in rhythm with his hand. She bit his lip, that copper taste forming. Her legs tightened, and she buried her face into his neck and shoulder and let out a loud, high moan that she tried to stifle it by taking a mouth full of his flesh. Using both of her hands, she grabbed onto his wrist as he continued to move inside her, holding him in place. Her body moved in short, quick shakes. Sweat beading her hairline and clavicle. Annie covered her face, embarrassed, and all Dan could see was a smile rising under her hand. She looked at him and bit the knuckle of her finger, laughing and giggling.

Dan felt on fire and hoped she did too. He was scared that it was all going to be over now, with that out of her system—that the booze might start to leave her through the sweat they worked up, and she'd be horrified at what they were doing. She looked over at him again, then at the ceiling. Taking the knuckle out of her mouth, she covered her face again with both hands. Then she rolled over and grabbed the side of his face. She kissed him, her mouth falling open, the flick of her tongue.

"Come here," she said and pulled him on top, falling between her legs. They tugged off each other's pants, bathed in the colors from the TV, a cool night breeze coming in from the partially opened door. He wanted to ask her if she was sure, but was scared she'd get cold feet. Then they kissed again, and he felt her delicate hand guiding him.

5

THE DRYNESS IN HIS MOUTH WOKE HIM, and the sunlight stabbing his eyes made him want to vomit. Dan tried to use his hand to block out the light, but it made little difference. He felt Annie's warm skin as she lay half on him, naked and asleep. The sheet felt glued to his crotch, and he winced when he lifted it off himself. But that was all the movement he could muster. He wanted to soak it all in. Soak her in. Consume her. He smelled the shampoo and cigarettes in her hair, and felt the softness of her breasts as they pressed into him while she slept, the wetness of drool slicking his chest. He worked his fingertips over her back. The skin was smooth and soft, different than the other skin on her body. The TV was still playing on mute, but it hurt too much to look at. He drifted to sleep again, twitching himself awake with a quick, sharp snore, but it didn't seem to disturb Annie. The next time he dozed off, he dreamt of Jackie. The fat man pulled the trigger this time, making Dan jump so hard he brought Annie back to life. She arched her back in a stretch and wiped her spit off of him.

"Sorry," she said. Then she buried her face into his chest and tightened her half hug around him.

"Don't be," he said. He wished he had the courage to ask if she regretted anything between them, but was too afraid she did. "How are you feeling?"

"I feel good," she said. "I can't remember the last time I slept that deeply. I mean, I feel like death, but I also feel good." She stretched and yawned so hard it made her body tremble, and rested her chin on his chest to look at him. "If that makes sense."

"It does to me," he said, hoping she'd piece together that any good feeling he had was because of her. "My head is killing me. Would you judge me if I had a little hair of the dog?"

"Only if you don't share. Once we get straight, we can get some food. Just not from the diner. I hate going on my days off."

Dan couldn't help but wonder how her husband was feeling with her being gone all night and not showing any intention of going back soon. The thought of asking her all of this floated through his mind, but he held back. *Why ruin it,* he thought. They both sat up on the bed, rubbing their feet over the thin carpet. Her hand was on top of his, and she gave it a gentle squeeze. It hurt, but he didn't show it, because he didn't want her to take it away. They scooped their clothes off the floor, and Dan pushed the dresser so that the door closed all the way. He cracked open a beer, and the pop of the can made him wince. He chugged half of it without stopping and handed the rest over to Annie, who sipped it slowly, covering her nakedness with the clothes from the floor.

"I'm going to hop in the shower real quick."

"Me too," she said.

Dan assessed himself in the mirror—the bruising and swelling, the bandages. His hand was less swollen, but the purple of it was turning pink and green. He tried to make a fist with little success. He chewed three aspirins and got into the shower before turning on the water. The cold stream washed over him, aching his hand before it warmed up. Steam began to fog the room and the shower door, and through the hazy shower door he saw Annie sitting on the toilet, her hand shielding her eyes from the light before she flicked the switch off. She ran a sheet of toilet paper over herself and flushed, spiking the water cold for a moment. Annie stepped into the shower with him. He moved out of the way, and she wet her hair and let the spray fall over her face. They kissed, and the smell of beer leapt off their breath. He cupped her breast, the water falling over his fingers and down his hand as she groped at him. This only lasted a moment before they rested their foreheads together, and Dan apologized, saying his head was hurting too much. Annie chuckled, then winced. She agreed and said she felt like she might get sick, so they finished the shower without fooling around anymore, only soaping each other up and stealing kisses.

Grease stained the bottom of the bag, making it wet and transparent—the best sign that it was exactly what they needed. They were both on their second sandwich, fried chicken with gravy between two biscuits. It made them feel sick and better at the same time. They shared a tall boy between them, wrapped in a paper bag. It was much easier for Annie to get beer this early in the morning, especially since the cashier was a man. Annie bought them each a cheap pair of sunglasses from the display on the counter as well, so they didn't have to keep squinting and shielding their eyes from the sun. They sat on the curb outside the fast-food place, tired from their walk. The plan was to drive, but Dan's car was dead from the headlights being on all night.

The dryness of the air sucked what little hydration they had left in them. At two different times on the walk, Annie needed to rest her hands on her knees and breathe deep, trying not to vomit. Dan finished his sandwich, wiped his mouth with the back of his hand, and reached into the bag for his third one. Annie balled up her wrapper and tossed it back into the bag, taking out a hash brown in a paper sleeve. She bit into it, and held out her hand toward Dan, who bent over and took a bite. Annie cleared her throat.

"We fucked up yesterday, didn't we?" she said through a long sigh.

Dan shrugged, unable to hide the hurt he forced into smile. "I was scared you'd think that."

"What? Oh hun, no," she reached out and put her hand on his. "I was talking about at the club. We never asked anyone about Lydia. That was the whole point."

Dan let out a laugh that was mostly air. "I didn't

even think about that." And that was the truth. He hadn't thought about Lydia since before the club. He thought of Jackie and his looming presence, but didn't give any thought to the other aspects of the arrangement.

Dan started speaking, unable to stop the words from coming out. Still, he didn't know if he even wanted to curb himself, especially since Annie put the reality of his remaining days into the ether again. "I don't know. I guess with everything that happened last night. The dancing and the, well, it all just felt so perfect. I didn't care really about anything else."

"That's so sweet," she said. "And I like hearing that. It's more complicated for me." She lowered her voice, talking to herself. *"Everything is always so complicated."* She turned to him and rubbed his leg. "I have a lot of things going on in my head right now, and I'm also trying not to throw up. I've been making myself not think about it too much, but when I do, I guess last night is the best I've felt since I can't even remember when. This is...it's nice and it's sweet...but it's also a hard pill to swallow. I don't know how to explain it."

"You don't need to explain. I hope you don't regret it."

She touched his arm. "I don't regret it at all. Which is why it's so complicated."

"It won't matter in a week anyway, it'll be our secret, and I'll take it to my grave."

"Maybe, but why not keep trying? We can go back again tonight, just no drinking this time."

"I asked this guy at a pawn shop if he knew her. He didn't, but he said to check out some local tattoo shops.

I mean, she could have gotten them years ago anywhere in the country. But if she ever lived with Jackie, there might be a good chance she got at least some locally."

"She's pretty, and with all of that modification, I'm sure she'd be memorable to someone. It's not a bad idea. Let's give it a shot."

Dan swallowed before he was done chewing. "Last night was great, but you don't have to keep—"

"Shush," she said, and playfully pushed his face away. "I'm not going anywhere just yet. We have a mystery to solve! But first, we need to go back to your place because I need some more sleep."

"What about your husband?" It was the first time he mentioned him so bluntly, no tiptoeing. It was weird and uncomfortable, but also liberating.

"It'll be a while before he cares that I'm gone. Plus," she put a sarcastic smile on her face and playfully punched Dan's arm, "He'll be alive next week, so that's a later problem." She grabbed the side of his face gently, moving a thumb over his eyebrow. "We should probably change this too."

"Let's go get some sleep."

He got up and wiped the sand and pebbles from the seat of his pants and helped Annie to her feet. She looked at him and stood on her tiptoes, kissing him gently on the lips. Back at the motel, they smoked a cigarette while sitting on the hood of his dead car, then went inside and both pushed the dresser against the door to close it tight. They undressed but were too tired and too sick, so Dan just curled up behind her like a spoon and fell asleep shortly after he felt her breathing get deeper and slower, and her body began to twitch.

In his dream, Dan was walking but never getting anywhere. His feet felt sluggish and sticky, like he was wading through mud, sinking deeper and deeper. The more he struggled, the more he sank. A silhouette appeared on the edge of the quicksand. Thin and slender, a slight hourglass, he thought it was Annie at first, relieved she found him. That she was going to save him. She held out her hand, but the hand was dark. Soft and delicate, a white palm, but the back of the hand, all the way up the arm, was tattooed black. She pulled him from of the mud. A fat, shadowy figure came lumbering out of the darkness. Instinctively, Dan grabbed the woman's hand and began to run, trying to pull her from the fat man. But the more he ran and the tighter he grabbed, the more the woman faded. The fear of losing her made him hold tighter and tighter until she was gone. Then he was sinking again. His legs wouldn't lift or move. He kept sinking, and any fight only pulled him down more.

Then there was Annie.

She walked out onto the mud, never sinking. He held out his hand, waiting for her to pull him to safety. But she didn't. She climbed down next to him, willing herself to sink into the mud. *Shh,* she said, gently stroking his face, getting close to him. She was in the muck but clean, as if standing in water. She kissed his cheek, below his eye, running her hand along the top of his head. *It's okay. It's all okay. I'm here. I'm not going anywhere. It's okay.* She turned and leaned into him, grabbing his hands and wrapping his arms around her. He buried his face in her neck. The shampoo and cigarettes were intoxicating. He felt like he was floating. In his mind, he was flying above them both. She reached for him and stroked his cheek. Dan didn't feel afraid anymore.

Annie's hand was on his cheek when he slowly opened his eyes. His hand was under her neck and reaching around to the front of her, cupping her breast. Her hair was lying across his face, her scent in his nose.

"You're awake," she said, thick with sleep.

"Yeah, I'm awake."

"It felt like you were having a nightmare."

"Half a nightmare, I'm okay." He squeezed her tight and she pressed herself into him. "What time is it?"

"About four," she said. "We should get up if we're going to get to some of those shops."

"Do we have to? This is too nice."

"That's why we have to."

6

THE ARGUMENT WITH DAN'S NEIGHBOR ended shortly after it started, before the two could fully get into shouting at each other. It was good that Annie was there to smooth things over and convince the man to help them jump Dan's car. The argument started because Dan asked the man for help, and the guy started laying into him about how his headlights were shining through his window all night. Dan probably could have apologized or at least acknowledged it in some way, rather than telling the guy to go to hell. He was an older Russian man who spat on the ground when Dan said this, raising his voice at Dan, who responded in kind.

Annie was a lifesaver.

"You should invest in some jumper cables," Annie said when it was all over and they got into the car. "Or one of those things that have a battery attached, so you can do it yourself without needing help."

"If I live past this week, I'll look into it."

Annie slouched in the seat and made a sound—an exasperated breath.

"What's wrong?" Dan put his phone on the dashboard with a map on the screen, leading them to different tattoo places.

"Nothing."

"Uh, it doesn't seem like it." He put his hand on her knee, and she lit a cigarette. She passed it to him and lit another one for herself.

"You're just always so, I dunno, flippant? Is that the word? Cavalier? Maybe that's better. So casual about talking about how you're going to die. You joke about it a lot."

"Does it bother you?"

"I don't think it's fair of me to say it's bothering me or ask you to stop. It's your life, and it's you know, your fate or whatever. It's just, I guess I don't always know how to respond."

"If I think about it too much, it really starts to fuck me up. Most days I'm only hanging on by a thread here. So, I crack jokes. What do they call that, like a mechanism, right?"

"Coping mechanism. It just makes me sad, is all." She looked out the window, ashing through the gap of space she cracked open. "I don't think I'm able to turn it off, even with jokes. I try, but it only makes me sadder." Her eyes welled up with tears, and she pressed her finger into the corner of her eyes by the bridge of her nose to try and cut them off at the pass. Her voice was weak and trembling now. "I don't want you to die, Dan."

"I don't want to die either." He cleared his throat. "Especially now." He put his hand on hers and squeezed it gently. "All we can do is just keep grinding away, you know?"

"Maybe we'll figure this out."

He shot her a grin, but the optimism was forced. "Yeah, maybe." They drove in silence the rest of the way to the first shop.

The first two places they went to were useless. No one there ever saw her. They let them flip through their albums, but Lydia and her tattoos weren't in any. After the second, they grabbed burgers from a drive-thru and ate them with the windows down while they smoked cigarettes and listened to an oldies station on the radio. The sun was setting, adding a low-hanging redness that deepened the maroon clay of the rocks, the cold air filling the vacuum left behind in the dwindling heat. A lump grew in Dan's throat, and he tried to cough it back. It all felt very classic, like if he closed his eyes, then opened them, maybe Annie would be in some poodle skirt, and he'd be wearing some leather jacket with grease in his hair. He didn't know what it meant or why it choked him up, but as he saw the sun setting, more than ever, he didn't want to die.

Maybe nobody ever wanted to die. Not really. Maybe Dan was just indifferent. He never gave it much thought until Jackie's fat finger pulled the hammer back. That's when he knew his life was all smoke contained within a bottle, fogging and filling it. It'd all be gone in a week. Annie wasn't even permanent—she'd be back with her husband. She couldn't be driving around with Dan forever, sleeping in his arms each night. She was mixed with the smoke slowly seeping from the seams of the bottle. There until she wasn't. Maybe if he was lucky, she'd stay the week. He was never lucky, though, and all the hope he had of finding Lydia was slipping through his fingers with each new place that shrugged their shoulders. He didn't even want to think about a happily ever after. He couldn't think of living past next week or filling himself with hope that he and Annie had a future. Hope was too dangerous right now, and Dan knew that.

"You knew Jackie in high school, right?" Dan jumped when Annie broke his concentration. "Sorry."

"Yeah," Dan said. He watched the sun sink lower, the reds turning to orange, to pink. Darkness hovering above it all.

"Was he always an asshole? Were you ever friends?" Annie shook her head with embarrassment. "I probably shouldn't be talking about this."

"No, it's fine," he said. "It's not like I wasn't thinking about it." Dan reached over between the seats and lightly twirled her hair in his fingers. She rested her head against his hand. "The school was small. So, everyone knew everyone. Everyone's parents were friends since they were in high school, and so it goes. We ran track together. He's a few years older than me. Also, yes, he was always an asshole."

"Is he really fat? Or are you just being mean?"

"Um, both, I guess. He's fat, but he wasn't always. He was an athlete at one time. Track star, football player. But then he got into an accident and broke his ankle and one of the other bones in his leg, I forgot which one. He couldn't do much for a while, so he just, well, became Fat Jackie."

"That's kind of sad."

"Maybe. It's hard to feel sympathy for him. He got a massive settlement, though. Which is how he got all his money. To his credit, l guess, he expanded it. But if you're already an asshole, and then you get rich that young and that fast. Just, boom, overnight—well, this is who you get."

"Dan, can I ask, and please don't get mad." She played with her straw, the plastic squeak filling up the car, "Why would you ever borrow money from a person like that?"

Dan took a deep breath and puffed it out his mouth. His exhale was followed by an *umm* as he tried to find the words. The thought, high-pitched and hesitant, betrayed any attempt to hide his embarrassment. "Because I'm an idiot."

"Besides that."

This made Dan laugh a burst of air from his nostrils. "Someone we went to school with, we never knew how to pronounce his real name, something like Gheorghe, his parents moved from Romania or the Balkans, one of those, we called him Georgio. I hadn't seen him in close to twenty years, maybe. I made okay money as a garbage man. It was enough. But when I saw how he was living—he said he was a stock guy, and I don't know anything about that shit.

"Who does?"

"He told me my money could make money. It was a lie. One of those schemes. And you ask yourself how someone could have been so dumb. Laughing at all those rich fucks on the news that fell for it. But, it works...for a time, that's the problem. You get money back. You get this growth, and it makes it seem so easy, but not so much that you're suspicious of it. I mean, I knew nothing, so when Georgio said he needed money, I got him money, and when he needed more to do more, I got him more. That's how I ended up borrowing from Jackie. I was so sure I'd be able to pay him back. Then Georgio disappeared, along with all my money."

"Maybe Jackie should be trying to find him."

"I think he might have gotten his hooks into Jackie, too, because his guys made it seem like Jackie...you know." He made an airy gunshot with his breath and pantomimed his head getting knocked back.

"Could they have just wanted to scare you?"

"Who knows? And then I borrowed more money to try and pay back what I owed, but that wasn't enough, and the only person I could borrow from was who I owed it to. I was desperate. I tried to bet horses, just to break even, and well—"

The thought trailed off unfinished. Annie went back to her drink, and Dan went back to watching the darkening sky. The car filled with silence again.

Dan's mind drifted into a daydream, and he watched all the sand and rocks melt away—the heat vapors turning into water. He pictured the two of them as the only living people in the world. Alone on an island somewhere. Not in a Gilligan's Island way with coconut phones and long straggly beards and pants torn into shorts. But them, living a normal life, only on an island. Seagulls and endless water around them. Waves crashing. Dan didn't even like the beach, but he liked the idea of nothing around them. Emptiness and silence, and no other living souls. Forever like that. Forever like this moment.

Dan cleared his throat softly, so he didn't completely shatter the comfortable silence surrounding them.

"What's that fishing called, the kind when they stand on the beach and have those real long poles," he said.

"What?" The word came out as a laugh.

"There's a type of fishing people do at the beach. They use these big rods, and even the lures are bigger." Dan estimated the size of the lure with his thumb and forefinger. "It'll come to me."

"I have no idea," said Annie . "I didn't even see the ocean until I was almost twenty. Why?"

"Whenever I'm thinking of a place, I always wonder what type of fishing they do there. What's that look?"

"That's really cute. I like learning these things," she said. "Are you a big fisherman? Is there a word for that?"

"An angler. And not really. My old man was. Not obsessed or anything, but it was just *his thing*. It was always so boring to me. I figured maybe I just didn't understand it. When you're young, relaxing is boring. He taught me a lot, and I still know it. Everything I learned—they're good memories. It's nice to think of him, too. I used to a lot more—dream of him, that is. Not so much, now. I don't know if that means anything, just time, maybe. Once you come to grips with how you'll never see them again, things get a bit easier, I suppose." Dan picked up Annie's cup and took a sip from the straw. The memories filled him with an emotion he couldn't place. Not melancholy, but not *not* that either. "I don't know how we got here, what was I talking about?"

"Fishing."

"I know how to fish, it's just nothing I cared about." Dan rested his head back on the headrest. "But then I got to thinking that maybe it's something you age into. One day, fishing finds you, and it all clicks. So, whenever I think of settling some place, I always wonder the fishing they do there."

"And you were thinking of the beach?"

"A bit, yeah—

The sun finished setting, and Dan drifted back into focus as Annie hit the bottom of her drink with her straw and the rattling of the ice, slurping up the last of the liquid. She held the empty fast-food bag open, and he put his wrappers in, wiping his mouth with his hand. She put her hand over his on the gear shift, her eyes warm and soft. He leaned over the center console and gave her a kiss.

The next tattoo shop was a twenty-minute drive filled with comfortable silence and singing along with the radio, punctuated by the voice of the GPS from his phone. The shop was almost identical to the others—vinyl checker squares on the floor, half walls separating the lobby from where the work was done, and each tattoo artist displaying their work in their respective stations. The place smelled of soap and rubbing alcohol, and ink. The buzzing of machines and needles was drowned out by the hard rock playing over the speakers. The woman behind the counter had a barbell going through the bridge of her nose and stretched earlobes, black and grey wings spread across her chest, up her neck and throat. Dan slid his phone across the glass counter top.

"We were wondering if you recognized this woman. Maybe she got some work done here."

"No, I'm sorry," she said.

The bottom dropped out of Dan's stomach. Annie looked at him with those apologetic eyes.

"But," the woman said, "I've only been here a few

months. Let me get one of the other guys. Hey Slate," she called behind her to one of the artists bent over a woman lying face down on a table with her shirt off and arms crossed under her head. The man sat up and looked toward the counter, sprayed a stream of green soap onto a paper towel and rubbed it over the woman's back, pulled off his gloves and tossed them into the can by his seat, before walking over to where Dan and Annie were waiting. "These people need to ask you questions about some girl."

"You guys cops?" Slate said.

"Man, come on." Dan gestured to the bruises on his face. They shared a laugh, and Annie rolled her eyes. "I'm trying to help a buddy find his daughter," he said, taking the phone off the counter and handing it to the artist. "Do you recognize this girl?"

Slate studied the photo on the phone for longer than Dan would have figured he needed. Lydia was pretty recognizable and, Dan assumed, just as unforgettable. The man looked younger than Dan, but the way he held the phone at arm's length away to see betrayed him.

"Goddamn it," Slate said. "I tell you, I can't see shit on these damn things."

"You can zoom in by—" Annie started to say before Slate cut her off.

"I know that." He pinched the screen, widening his fingers. "My eyes just ain't what they used to be, is all." The woman he was tattooing tried looking over her shoulder at her back. Slate continued studying the phone.

"That's a no, I take it?" Dan said.

"Yeah," Slate said.

"Thanks anyway." Dan took his phone back, shoulders slumped, and all his effort put into not curling up into a ball right there on the shop floor.

"No," Slate said, "sorry, *yeah,* as in *I've seen her before*. Not, *yeah,* as in *I don't know her.*" Dan was trembling with excitement. He tried to hide the shivers that ran through his body with each pulse. Annie grabbed his hand, both of them hanging on every word. "I just couldn't remember where I knew her from. She might have been in here before. I think one of my guys used to get with her, maybe that's how I know her. You spend that much time with someone doing all that work. It was years ago, though, but we can see. Johnny Boy." He called toward the back of the shop, hands cupped around his mouth like a megaphone. A skinny man with sunken eyes came out of the back room, a sandwich in his hand and mustard in the corner of his mouth. He wiped it with his fingers, then rubbed it on his jeans. He was pale, and his black hair made him look paler. "Johnny Boy, who was that girl you used to go with a few years ago, with the body mods?"

"Need more than that," he said, chuckling through the bite he had squirreled into the corner of his mouth.

"The one with all the black work. Didn't she split her tongue, too? Here," he held his hand out to Dan, who gave the phone back to him, "this chick."

"Yeah, Lydia."

A wave of relief washed over Dan. He felt like he could breathe again.

"I haven't seen her in years, though."

Dan lost the feeling.

"Is she okay?"

"We're not sure," Annie said. "She's missing and we're trying to find her. Do you have any ideas?"

"Me and her only hooked up a few times, was never anything serious, sorry," he said, and took another bite.

Dan took the phone back and put it in his pocket. He and Annie gave each other the same knowing look with their half-crooked smiles. There was no optimism, both realizing that they put too much goddamn hope into this plan without realizing it.

"But," the kid said, swallowing a bite so big and quick it made him wince, "like I said, me and her used to hook up. After me, she was with Jimmy the Saint, I know that. He was a real asshole, but that was a long time ago. I thought I heard that maybe she was fooling around with Quick Rich, but I don't know how true that is. Slate, did you ever hear of them together?"

"How would I know? Fuck that guy," Slate said, looking up from the woman he was tattooing. "I bumped into him the other day. I still hate that mother fucker. I almost beat the shit out of him right there outside the drug store. Quick Rich can suck my quick dick."

Dan laughed. "Hell of a nickname these guys got. Jimmy the Saint?"

"They're all ironic," Johnny Boy said.

Annie cleared her throat. "Would you happen to know where we could find Jimmy?"

"No, sorry. The last I heard, he was tending bar at a club a few towns over. Not a DJ kind, the kind with live bands. Metal bands, punk bands. It's a shit hole."

"The Monkey's Paw?" Annie asked.

"That's the one," Johnny Boy said, taking another bite.

"Son of a bitch," Dan said, a stunned look on his face.

"What?" said Slate.

"We were just there last night."

"Maybe you saw Jimmy the Saint then—tattoos, bald, good-looking dude."

"Mother f—" The rest of the word came out as a wheezy laugh of disbelief as Dan rubbed his forehead with his good hand.

"Thank you so much," Annie said. "This was such a big help."

"Glad to hear it." Johnny Boy rubbed his hands on his jeans and shook their hands.

Back in the car, Dan and Annie started screaming in excitement. He pounded the steering wheel repeatedly, not caring about the pain shooting up his arm.

"We were right there!"

"I know!" Annie said.

"Your thinking was spot on!" Dan grabbed her face and gave her a cartoonish kiss on the lips, with the real heavy smacking sound—the kiss he wanted to give her in the bathroom at the diner. "I'd be lost without you!"

Annie was smiling and smiling hard, from one ear to the other. She shrugged her shoulders and shimmied with excitement.

"Should we head there now?" Annie asked.

"I'm down if you are."

"Let's go!" Annie said. Excitement filled the car like helium, making him feel like they could float away.

"Surf casting!"

Annie looked at him blankly.

"The type of fishing from before—never mind."

As Dan backed out of the parking spot and turned onto the main road, he heard Annie's phone buzz inside her pocket. She looked at it, grimaced, and put it back in her pocket. She said nothing, but the car didn't feel as light.

The club had fewer people in it than the night before, but it was still early. Dan was glad to be out of the car. Even though the drive was only twenty minutes, it was a long twenty minutes. He and Annie didn't speak the whole ride. The car wasn't silent—they had the radio on, and they weren't strangers to each other either. They still passed cigarettes back and forth, and she rested her hand on his thigh as they drove, but it was different. A thick tension flooded the car when she got that text and trapped them both underwater, crushing them, quietly drowning. The noise from the club gave Dan some comfort knowing there would be no more silence, and when they talked it would be loud and close. Dan figured it was her husband calling and texting, buzzing away in her pocket. She would silence and shoot Dan another apologetic look. *It's complicated*, she said to him earlier, but she never explained how. Her look reinforced the statement. She grasped his hand as they walked into the club, slipping her arm through his and hugging it close to her chest. The bartender was standing behind the bar, leaning back with his arms crossed, listening to the band on stage banging trash cans and smashing guitars.

"Are you Jimmy the Saint?" Dan asked as they pulled up their stools.

"Amaretto and a Boilermaker, right? And it's just James now, none of that 'Saint' shit. I don't do that stuff anymore. Been almost eight months."

"Congrats," Dan said.

"That's so great," Annie echoed, both shouting over the music. "James, do you know this girl?"

He took the phone and only needed to glance at the photo. "Lydia? Yeah, we dated for a while. She in trouble?"

"We're not sure, but we hope not," Dan said.

"When's the last time you saw her?"

James tossed down two coasters and placed their drinks on them, not needing the book to make Annie's drink this time.

"I haven't seen her in eight months." He paused and gave a shrug. " She left for a reason."

"You haven't seen her at all since then?" Annie said.

"No. She started going around with this kid from New York, some guy called 'Dusa, because of his dreadlocks. I don't know his real name, though. Had a scar by his eye, if that helps? But I haven't heard from them since. They went to New York for a bit, I think, but I don't know if that's true."

"Damn," Dan hammer-fisted the bar top in frustration. "Do you know of anyone else who might have seen her?"

"No, I don't talk to anyone from those days anymore. Can I get you guys anything else?"

Her voice thick with defeat, Annie asked, "Have you ever heard the name Quick Rich?"

"I'll take another beer," Dan said.

"Never heard that name before," James said.

Annie said, "If she wasn't in New York, if she was still around here, do you know of any place she might be? An old apartment or an old job? Friends? Anything that might help?" He took Annie's glass, then paused.

"There is a place up north that she loves," James

said. "By T-or-C. This hike she goes on. You wouldn't think it to look at her, but she loves that shit. Being outside and hiking. She took me there once. Another time, she disappeared to there for about three days and came back as if nothing happened. She loves that place. It's not much, but I guess it's the only thing I can think of. This isn't new, the whole no one can find her thing you have going on. She's just like that."

"Do you remember how to get there?" Annie asked.

"No, she drove. I was pretty out of it back then."

"Here," Dan said, sliding his phone, "do you think you could find it on a map? At least ballpark it?" Dan rotated the phone on the bar so James could see it better. He called up a map and zoomed in with his fingers to Truth or Consequences.

James looked at the phone and started swiping through the area, following the roads and the river. He zoomed in closer. "Right around here, I'd say. Up in these hills somewhere. She loves the view, so it's up high."

"This was a big help," Annie paid for the drinks and tipped almost the cost of the tab. "Thank you."

Outside of the bar, the wave of mixed emotions showed clearly on their faces. They were excited to have any sort of lead, although the hope was starting to weigh on Dan, and he wished he didn't have it. Any of it. But that excitement was only short-lived because Annie's phone kept buzzing, and they both knew what that meant. Annie leaned against his car, cigarette between her fingers, chewing her lower lip with anxiety.

"Dan," she said, a small quiver in her voice. "I need to go home tonight. I'm sorry. It's just that—"

"Annie, I knew what this was from the jump."

"Dan," she said his name again, and it struck him that she was repeating it each time she spoke. Focused on having his attention. The first one wavered with anxiety, but this one had an exhaustion to it. It weighed heavy. "I don't know what this is. I really don't. You said you do. You weren't some, you *aren't* just some sort of—"

"Pity fuck."

"Yes. Please let me talk."

Dan went to apologize, but knew he'd be interrupting her again. He rubbed his hand through his hair, messing it up with his nervous energy, embarrassed. He held out his bad hand toward Annie, who passed him the pack of cigarettes. He inhaled, and a shiver ran through his body, coughing slightly.

"I don't know what this is," Annie said, with a calmness that tried to reset the moment. "We were both drunk but not drunk enough to not know what we were doing. And I've been with you all day. I wasn't drunk this morning in the shower either. Clearly, there is something here. And I like you, Dan. *I do.* I don't know when it started, but that's the truth. Do you think I help all my customers bandage their faces? You can say you knew what this was from the jump and that's good for you. Congrats. Do what you need. I know this thing... *us, this,"*—she gestured openly around her to encompass everything. "It's all very complicated and weird. And trust me, I wish I could just stay with you and help you. And I wish Trevor wasn't blowing up my phone this whole goddamn night. I don't know what I'm walking into when I get home."

Dan's face contorted with anger.

"No," she said. "Nothing like that. He's not going to

hit me. He'd never. I'm just saying, fuck, I don't know what I'm saying, Dan. Why am I telling you all of this? I don't tell anyone this shit. I didn't even drink that much. What is happening? *Fuck*."

She dropped her cigarette onto the pavement and worked it into the ground with her foot. Dan flicked his butt across the parking lot. Annie, trembling, lit another one for herself.

"Things with Trevor aren't great, and they haven't been for a while. He's a good guy. Sorry if that hurts, but he is. It's just we're strangers now. We haven't touched each other in months. Not even kisses hi and bye, nothing. Half the time, he sleeps on the couch. He'll know what happened as soon as I walk in. You and him seem to know more about what I'm doing than I do, apparently. So, it's complicated. And no, I don't regret last night. And I'm going to help you find this girl. Because we will find her, and we'll get you out of this. It'll make everything even more fucked up and confusing, but we'll do it. Because we have to. I can deal with confusing, but I can't deal with you being dead."

Annie's voiced trailed away, and she started to cry, burying her head in her hands while she stood against his car, sobbing. Dan wrapped his arms around her, but she tensed and said, "Please don't," through the sobs in her hands. Dan let go of her and leaned against the car next to her, close enough that their hips touched. She stood there crying, and he stood there smoking, studying the painting of the Monkey's Paw logo.

* * *

In the car, she held his hand in silence on the gear shift as they drove to the diner where her car was still parked, sitting alone in the lot.

"It kind of felt good to get all that out," she said. "I can't say I feel better, but I'm glad I said something. What are you going to do now?"

"Head up north, I guess, check out the area he pointed out. I have no other leads. I'll go tomorrow, though. Tonight, I'm going to go home and be sad for a while."

"Don't do that," she said. Her face was hurt and frustrated at the same time. "Don't put that on me."

"I didn't mean it like that. There isn't any other way to put it. I need to try and come up with some sort of plan since my current one is just wandering through the desert hoping to run into a girl I've never seen before, in a place I've never been before. So, I'm just going to go home, drink, and sulk for a bit and hopefully wake up with all of that out of my system."

"Will you text me tomorrow and let me know how you make out?"

"I'm not going to make out with her, she's half my age, you creep."

This made Annie laugh, relieved at the broken tension. "Thank you."

They looked at each other with hesitation. They touched their cheeks and made a kissing sound. Then she left. He watched her get into her car and waited until she drove off. He followed until he had to turn off toward the motel. He wanted to kiss her goodnight—maybe it was even goodbye—but something didn't seem right. Something about kissing a girl on the mouth and sending her home to her husband. Dan made himself laugh out loud with the thought of why this goodbye felt wrong, given the night they spent together.

He couldn't explain it, it just did.

7

THE DRIVE WAS LONG AND DULL. ONLY bare desert and miles of nothing. Occasionally he'd pass a chile field with workers bent low, backs arched as they moved up and down their rows, pump jacks methodically nodding behind them along the horizon. The rest was just sand and rocks and shrubs. Clear blue skies though. Dan got a later start than he planned to because he slept like shit. He had too much to drink and couldn't rein in his mind. He couldn't escape the thoughts, even now driving. If he focused on why he was so tired, he thought of how he didn't sleep and of the thoughts that kept him awake all night, and now the thought of those thoughts just reminded him of everything he was trying to block out. It never ended.

Last night, he was plagued by constant thoughts of Annie and her husband together in bed. Because he knew what she was like—what she looked like, and felt like, her scent. Dan couldn't stop his mind. Her husband gasping out to God under his breath when she did that thing with her tongue. She said they were strangers, that they don't touch each other, but maybe they do. Maybe she was just trying to make him feel better. Annie and Trevor could make up. What if he knew what she was doing last night and today and knew he was losing her? Then when she came home, he'd lay on the charm and have flowers ready, they'd drink wine, and he'd scatter rose petals on the bed. He'd be crying, and she'd be crying, and then they'd comfort and hold each other. They would kiss, and it would lead to them rekindling everything they had. She'd lie in bed afterwards and she'd think of Dan and what they did, and she'd regret it, if she didn't already.

All night, Dan sat in the unlit hotel room and looked at himself in the dark reflection of the TV. Seeing himself sitting against the backboard, legs out in front of him, crossed at the ankles, beer in hand, just watching his darker self drink. Only losing sight of himself for a moment when his head would tilt back to take a swig from his can, dropping each empty one onto the floor. He did this again until he lost count. He took two big gulps of gut rot from a plastic jug, and passed out face down, still in his jeans and sneakers.

But sleep offered him no relief, just Jackie blowing his brains out on a loop like a broken film projector. He knew he was dreaming, but he couldn't wake himself. He saw a movie once as a kid where a man was strapped to a chair and his eyes were forced open, and he was made to watch violence on a big screen until he got himself sick. They'd keep going for days or weeks, and he'd be screaming and crying. This was Dan now—strapped down in his dream, forced to watch Fat fucking Jackie and his fat fucking fingers sending bullets through Dan's stupid fucking face over and over. Only stopping long enough for the image of a man with a blurred face fucking Annie until she was clawing at his back and quivering in ecstasy. Jackie bigger than ever, laughing and laughing, his fat fucking stomach bobbing up and down. Dan would beg for death, to be put out of his misery, and Jackie would cackle at him and refuse.

Then the loop would start over.

He finally woke himself out of sheer will and felt the relief of his surroundings, his sense of direction returning. It was dark out, still the middle of the night. He tried to stay awake, scared to fall back into that abyss, but sleep overtook him. The new dreamscape didn't have Jackie in it, or Annie either. Just Lydia. Lydia, with her arms outstretched, the black ink covering them down to the fingers, walking backwards, reaching for Dan to grab her. To help her. But he never could. No matter how hard he tried, he couldn't gain on her, unable to bridge that hair-thin space between their fingers.

Dan woke with drool on his pillow and bees in his head, and a belly full of bile wanting to escape his mouth. He was able to choke it down and chew a few aspirins. It was only a medium hangover, he could navigate that. All the same, he drank his last tall boy and lay back on the bed. This time, he turned on the TV. He flipped through the stations until he found the most engaging and mindless thing to put on—just another report about that Wall Street asshole that was found dead. Dan sat there in a daze of apathy and sickness, looking at the screen but not watching. He wondered if the guy was anything like Georgio. Then he wondered about the odds of two stock market guys getting killed so close together, assuming Jackie did shoot Georgio in the face like his goons said. Maybe it happened more than he realized, and it just stuck out to him now because he was in the middle of it. Like how you never see your car on the road until you buy it, then it's everywhere. Or maybe the guy was asking for it, just like Georgio was.

It was four o'clock by the time he got up, changed his shirt, and grabbed his car keys.

Dan hadn't heard anything from Annie all day. Not that he tried to reach out either, but he wasn't the one who left last night. It weighed on him all morning, checking his phone during every commercial break of the shows he wasn't watching, and now between songs on the radio he wasn't listening to, the signal dropping in and out. The static and the rhythm of the highway hypnotized him. Every so often, a lizard would run across the road, and Dan would realize that he couldn't remember the last few miles he had driven. He didn't know why, but he found his mind wandering through his past—he wished the memories were happier, but mostly it was a flood of instances that made him wince. He'd remember snapping at his old man or teasing his sister so much she cried. Gagging on his grandma's pesto when she accidentally doubled the garlic, and it made her cry and lock herself in the bathroom. Maybe this was one of the steps he learned about after his dad died. DABsomething. Denial, X, Y, Z, and Acceptance, that's all he remembered, that time was a blur for him. But maybe somewhere in the middle was this. Where the mind ended up when the finish line was in sight, knowing there was more behind than in front. For Dan, the finish line wasn't tape spread across a road like a race well run, but rather a pistol with a bullet that cost ten thousand dollars.

Dan thought of his dad and of his dad's dad. He couldn't help but compare himself. Matching them drink for drink. Except that Dan was able to function, or at least he used to. It was all a haze, now. He had a good life before Georgio dangled the possibility of more in front of him, didn't he? He woke up every morning feeling like shit but still made it to work, still saved his money. Had a place. Dan found that all the memories of his dad were polished clean of any dirt now that he was gone. Not that he had been an angel, but the things that bothered Dan when he was alive didn't carry that same weight now. Things were just things. Moments just moments. Actions lost their malice and intention—everything made more sense. In his memories, it was okay that his dad was human, and Dan just hoped people would look at him the same way when Jackie was through with him. Scrubbed close to sainthood.

On the way out of town, he stopped at a gas station to fill up and bought himself two hard-boiled eggs in plastic packaging and some beef jerky. He also bought two Red Bulls, an orange soda, and another tall boy for the road. He drank half the beer while he pumped the gas, poured out half the soda, then filled the rest of the bottle with beer. He was nearing the pin on the map of his GPS with the sun getting lower, filling the skies with pinks and reds and some oranges that ran razor-thin along the horizon. He finished the jerky and polished off the eggs, washing them down with the beer mix. Up ahead of him, rising from the ground, growing larger as he got closer, was a steeple. A rugged-looking church, maybe a barn at one time, just brown wood and rot, and sloppy paint. It looked close to being condemned, but it was active, at least according to the sign out front. Black letters printed on clear plastic pushed together to make the words THE HOLINESS OF THE APOSTLES CHURCH, and underneath FAITH WILL DELIVER YOU SAFE. The lights were on and the front doors open, but the inside looked empty as he drove by.

When he arrived at the spot on the map, he still had some daylight left. The redness of the evening sent a cool wind whirling around him when he got out of his car, running a chill down his spine and putting a quiver in his stomach. His eyes adjusted to the dusk quickly, and he used the light on his phone to find the path that cut through the shrubs and bushes. The loose gravel and stones gave him unsteady footing in the sand as he walked, tripping and stumbling and rolling his ankles. He wasn't even half a mile into his walk before his sneakers were filled with rocks. He had no idea what he was looking for or what he was expecting—that he'd walk upon her sitting at a campfire or some shit, roasting marshmallows and smoking a joint? Maybe a note pinned to a rock that said Lydia was here, and now she's there. But this was his only option. Otherwise, he'd be sitting home drinking himself numb, probably digging a thumb into his eyebrow to see if it was still open, testing the movement in his hand, trying to squeeze a fist until the deep burning ripped through his arm. Maybe just put on some porn and jerk off into the toilet. Anything to take his mind off this.

Anything to take his mind off Annie.

It was as if all the sand in Dan's hourglass was slipping through Fat Jackie's trigger finger and all he cared about was that Annie wasn't with him. Alone in the goddamn desert chasing his tail. It was so dark he didn't know why he was even out there. Why did he get such a late start? Fucking moron. Dan wondered if Annie thought of him at all. Probably not now that he was out of sight and she was wrapped up in her husband's arms, his face in her neck. She'd forget that Dan even existed. God, why was he going through this whole song and dance? Why not just take matters into his own hands, achieving the same outcome but not giving Jackie the satisfaction? Somehow manage to get the money, all of it, put it in a duffel bag and drop it right at Jackie's feet, then blow his own fucking face off right in front of him, just because. Dan knew his brain was in upside down right now, and sometimes it felt good to let it go to the dark places. But there had been more than one time over the last few days that he knew it was a good thing he didn't own a gun.

An awful smell encompassed Dan like a thick mud as he continued down the trail. He couldn't escape it. He lifted his shirt over nose, but it did nothing. The scent made him sick to his stomach, but he kept moving towards it. He heard a ruffling in the bushes, movement and air, getting louder the stronger the scent got. He passed his light over the sand and rocks, scanning the darkness, then stopped. Dan halted his beam on the glass-like eyes reflecting back at him. A large bird, its head bald and red like a turkey emerging from its turtleneck of feathers, stood on a dead animal concealed by shadows and bushes, and darkness. The bird returned to its meal, others dancing alongside it, looking for a spot to grab a bite.

Dan walked closer to the birds, holding his hand over the shirt that already covered his nose and mouth. He ran the light along the ground, then focused on the carcass the bird was standing on. It wasn't an animal. The large bird's talons were clutching the torso of a person. Long hair, matted and twisted with dirt and blood. Chunks of scalp gone. One of the eyes was missing, part of the cheek eaten away. Teeth showing like a smile on the wrong side of their face. Below that, the skin was tan and red from the sun. Then black. All black. A black tattoo ran around the corner of their face, beneath the ear. The blackness worked down the side of the face, covering the neck and throat, onto the chest. The shirt, ripped apart, framed the body's right breast, which was gone—only fat seeping from the missing tissue. The body stopped abruptly below the stomach. The rest was eaten away. Maybe coyotes. A bird had its head in the hollow of the ribcage, pulling out anything left inside.

A sudden rage came over Dan, and he searched under his feet with his light, picking up the biggest stones he could find. Each rock that went sailing through the air sent more birds flying away. Some took more than one before they budged. A smaller vulture spread its wings and vomited toward Dan, rotten meat tossed close to ten feet, splattering by his shoes. Dan ran at the bird, swearing and kicking dirt until it finally left. The birds were gone, but the smell remained, circling Dan in a dark cloud. And doom rolled in like thunder, the static gathering and charging, waiting to strike from inside the thick stench.

Dan walked to the body on the ground and flashed his light on the remains.

Lydia.

He fell to his knees and vomited into the sand. Eggs and jerky and beer, acid and bile, his whole life spilling from him, dripping from his nose and the tears rolling down his cheeks. Lydia lay in the sand, half-devoured by the wilderness and all the dangers it brought. Lying there with her were the remaining days of Dan's life—all just bird shit and vulture vomit. And soon he'd be bleaching in the sun alongside her, feeding the desperate, hungry animals of the desert.

8

THE SMELL STILL LINGERED IN HIS NOSE even back in the car. He punched the steering wheel as he drove, the brightness of the flash still burning white and hot in his mind. The picture frozen on the screen. Pale film over her remaining eye, and teeth peeking through her cheek. The darkness was darker than he'd ever seen before, looming and black, surrounding his car. The stench made him retch as he drove. He turned on the overhead light, lifting his leg to check his pants. He didn't see anything, so he reached down and pulled off one of his sneakers. He sniffed the bottom of his shoe and immediately started coughing. He threw the sneakers out the window and into the darkness, the cool air filling the car and sucking the smell out. He tossed his socks out too.

Dan pulled the car to the side of the road to vomit again. He looked at the picture on his phone. Dan leaned his head against the rest, and pinched the bridge of his nose, trying to beat back the headache he knew was beginning to sneak in behind his eyes. It felt as if the car was filling up with water, and Dan began to breathe faster and faster, sweat leaking down his forehead. Jackie's hand wrapped tighter around his neck. Dan didn't even realize he was crying. He texted *Annie We need to talk. Something happened* and tossed the phone on the passenger seat. The drive through the dark, winding desert was a fog in his mind—no memory of the road behind him, and no attention to the road ahead of him. A light was glowing in the distance, growing as it got closer, a light from heaven. A gas station.

The tile, flat and smooth, was cold on Dan's bare feet. The person behind the counter might have said something to him about not wearing shoes, but Dan didn't hear it or care. He put a six-pack of beer on the counter and pointed to a pack of cigarettes, the same type that Annie smoked.

"Do you have anything stronger than beer?" Dan asked.

"Not anymore. Not since that damned law made us choose between liquor or gas," the man behind the counter said.

"My fucking luck." Dan rubbed his palm over his face. "Any chance *you* have something stronger than beer?"

The man took a deep breath, leaned over the counter, and looked at the empty parking lot. Dan's car sat alone under the flickering fluorescent lights. The man scratched his chin, debating internally. He shrugged and walked along the counter to a door that led to a back room. He appeared a minute later with two nip bottles of Fireball.

"Here," the man said. "We got stuck with a shit ton

of these bottles we can't sell no more. Government's a bunch of goddamn crooks. Take 'em."

"Here," Dan added a few more bucks to his total.

"Keep your money. Just pay for this shit here."

"You sure?"

"Man, I only work here. I don't give a fuck if you stole everything off the shelves." The man put everything in a paper bag.

"Don't mind if I do," Dan joked and pocketed a lighter from the display. The man simply shrugged, reached into his back pocket, and pulled out a flask.

"Here's to better luck," he said and took a swig.

Dan sat in the back seat of his car, door open and legs outside, the grit and pebbles of the rough pavement digging into his feet. He finished the nip bottles—chugging the first one and sipping the next—then downed two beers back-to-back before peeling the plastic from the cigarettes, and banging the pack on his wrist twice. The wrapper danced and rolled across the parking lot, tumbling over itself until it disappeared into the blackness of the night. His nervous energy channeled through his mind and body, down his arm, where it escaped through his thumb as it worked back and forth over the stiff filter of his cigarette. The cherry fell between his feet and bounced around until it went out. He tried to relight it but gave up and flicked the butt into the darkness and lit a new one. His mind was both blank and racing so fast that the blur made it as if he were thinking about nothing—only Lydia's pale blank eye staring at him, and the smell of the birds.

Down the dark street, a light pierced the sky. Dan could see it from the backseat of the car as he polished off his fourth beer out of the six. He stood unsteady and leaned against the car until he got his legs back, then walked to the light like a moth, the roughness of the road cutting into the bottom of his feet. The light came from the church he passed earlier. The parking lot was still empty, but now the lights were turned on throughout the building, punctuating the night with a sickly yellow glow. Dan peeked through the crack of the partially opened door and saw a man with his back to him arranging the wooden pulpit at the front of the room, rows of wooden benches to either side of him. Cases lined the wall behind the man, each covered in a dark cloth, bright, hot spotlights shining down on them. Dan finished his beer and took a quick look around, his vision floating behind his mind, delayed and rushing to catch up to the movement of his head. Seeing no garbage, he chucked the empty can into the bushes that lined the front of the church and went inside. He tried to be quiet, but the bench squeaked when he sat down, and the man at the front of the room turned to him.

"You're a bit early for the service. You're free to wait," he said, walking to where Dan sat. The man wore a flannel shirt tucked into his jeans, loafers, and a braided belt with his cellphone clipped to it. "Son, are you in trouble?" he asked, looking at Dan with the green and yellow bruises on his face, a discolored hand, barefoot, and stinking of beer.

"I believe so," Dan said, eyes glazed and having trouble focusing. "It's got me real good this time." He rubbed his hands over his face. "No one can help, Father."

"You don't have to call me that. I'm not a priest. Are you sure there is nothing I can do for you? Where are your shoes?" The man had a thick southern accent, somewhere from deep in the south, somewhere like Kentucky, or Alabama, maybe Mississippi.

"I got rid of them. They smelled," Dan's head was spinning as he looked around the room, momentarily forgetting where he was. "What kind of church is this? I've never been to something like this before."

"We're a Pentecostal church."

"I don't know what that is. Usually, it's all stone and marble and stained glass with sad faces and Jesuses nailed to shit."

"We believe salvation is given to us by a faith in Jesus. We believe in the healing power of his blood and of the Holy Spirit." He lifted his eyes toward the rafters and held his arms as if he was cradling a bowl. "We believe in signs and miracles and that we can do all things through His holy name. And that our faith will deliver us safely from harm."

"Faith will deliver you from harm?" Dan's words slurred. "Then you don't know Fat Jackie, do you, Father. Ain't a force on Earth or in Heaven, shit, Hell even, can deliver you from his wrath. And believe me, Lord, it's coming my way."

"Is that what brings you to our service this evening? Deliverance from this," a quizzical look crossed his face, "Fat Jackie?"

"I don't know why I'm here. I'll tell you what I do know, though—I know that I am drunk. I know that I don't have much longer on this Earth. And I know," he hung his head between his legs and took a deep breath, "and I know that I am exhausted. I just need a place to rest right now, is all. I'll get going."

"Don't be so hasty. You're free to stay as long as you need. Others will be coming soon. Please stay and join us. Maybe we can talk more afterwards if you'd like. Will you stay?"

Dan didn't want to, but he was tired, down to his bones. All he wanted was to close his eyes and sleep forever. He couldn't have left if he wanted to—his head was too light, his eyelids were too heavy, and his feet were too stuck. He nodded to the man and slouched down in the bench so he could rest his head on the wooden back of the pew. His eyes were closed and he felt the weight of the bench shift as the priest got up and was walking to the pulpit again. The sounds and smells of the room faded into nothing, then the lights, and Dan felt as if his head was melting into the wood. Then he was gone.

He didn't even dream.

Dan woke with a start to all the hoopin' and hollerin' going on around him. The room was filled with people he didn't hear come in. They were all chanting now and jumping and shaking. Some were weeping, and others were speaking in a mumbled gibberish, crying to the ceiling in a strange language. A man fell over, and the woman next to him began fanning herself. The priest was now up front, pacing behind the pulpit, sweating, and wiping a cloth along his forehead and neck. Punching at the wooden stand with each point he was hammering home.

The crowd responded in a chorus of *Amens* and *Yes Lords*.

"And we know," he said, more shouting than speaking. "We know that our faith in God will be rewarded.

Our faith in God will deliver us!" His accent came out heavy on the word *God*, the tone dipping and elongating every time he said it. *Gauud.* "And we know there is a crown a-waiting for us. With jewels. Y'all like that? Like the sound of that? A big shiny crown with jewels the likes we've never seen! The jewels that show off *our* heavenly reward. Show *our* glory! And, we know that with *our* faith we will be delivered, we know that with *our* faith *we* will be kept safe. That none can harm us!" He punched the wood between every statement. "*We cannot be harmed!* Let me hear you say it!"

"We cannot be harmed," their staggered response to his call, excited but clumsy.

"The devil has no hold on us! I said, *the devil* has *no hold* on *us!* I said, his head was crushed. Was it not? By the good Lord Jesus hisself! He stomped on that ol' devil, and crushed the serpent! *Crushed* him, did he not?"

"Yes, he did, Lord," they responded.

Dan was still drunk. The room wasn't spinning, but it was rocking back and forth like the hull of a boat, sounds pulsing in waves. He didn't know what anyone was talking about. He felt like he couldn't move.

"When Paul was bitten by the serpent, was he scared? *I said,* was he scared of that ol' asp? Was he!"

Their collective *no*s sounded like *boo*s.

"With faith, we shall be able to handle snakes, and they will not bite us. Their poison has no effect. That's what the Gospel of Mark says! When we are in the hands of the *Almighty God*, they can-not-harm-us. Our faith *will* deliver us safely." As he said this, he ripped the dark cloth off the box behind him, and the lights of the room caught the glass case, striking it as if it were glowing. In the tank, a large rattle began to hiss, the sound filling up the room, growing as it bounced off the walls and knocked around in Dan's brain. The mumbled language of the crowd got louder and louder as the man opened the lid of the case, reaching inside, and grabbed the snake. He held it in his hand, and Dan watched the snake wrap itself around his arm, the tail never stopping. "Through my faith, I am delivered! The serpent has no hold on me!" He held the snake up high for the crowd to see, and the roar of the jumbled prayers filled the room with a tremor. "Who among you wants to prove their faith? Who wants to testify how the Holy Spirit is in you, keeping you safe? Who among you has that mustard seed of faith? To walk and not sink? Who? Come forward! Show us your faith!"

A young woman, dancing and shouting, raised her hands and walked to the pulpit. She was lively, which Dan found jarring because of her mousy look—the cardigan sweater and long skirt, white socks sticking out of her bulky brown clogs. She was sweating and twitching with the Holy Spirit, keeping her eyes to the ceiling as she took the snake from the pastor and held it in her hands, high above her head. She shouted her thanks to God and her amens, and she started to shuffle in place, dancing, twirling.

Dan didn't see what happened, he just heard the crowd gasp. Then the scream. When he looked up, the woman was yelling in hysterics with the snake latched onto her face. When she tried to drop the snake, it hung there for a moment before falling. She grabbed her cheek and was panicking for God to help her. But it wasn't a prayer. Everyone stood in shock as the woman's face swelled. She was audibly gasping for air and waving her arms out to people, trying to grab them. The priest jumped from the pulpit and chased the snake as it slithered through the crowd. Dan remembered his bare feet and lifted them onto the bench. Members from the church ran to the woman who was now on the ground, and they all held their hands out over her, mumbling in their prayer language. People called out *Her faith will deliver her, her faith will keep her safe.* The preacher came back with the snake held high above his head, holding it up to the crowd, the damn thing's rattle still going a mile a minute.

"If we believe!" the man shouted. "Then nothing can harm us. If we believe! Then this venom has no power over us!"

A small group of people were still kneeling over the mousy woman, the rest turned their attention to the preacher with the snake and his shouting, and they called back, jumping and shaking. A chill slithered through Dan, rattling his insides, and he looked to see if anyone was calling for an ambulance, but didn't see any phones out. He reached into his pocket and felt only his thigh. He quickly checked around him and the floor under his seat, but found nothing. The heat and excitement sobered Dan up, but he was still exhausted. All he wanted to do was sleep, but no peace was to be found here anymore. The noise faded into a blur in the background as Dan walked out the doors and into the darkness again. He didn't realize how hot it had gotten in the church until he was outside walking to his car with the coolness of the night blowing across his face and climbing up his legs from the cold, rough pavement.

The door to the back seat of his car was wide open, the overhead light still on. The rest of his beer sat on the ground by the back tire. Empty cans lay on their sides next to the remaining beers, still connected by their plastic rings. Dan sat in the back seat and opened another beer, flashes of the mousy girl pleading for help through her swollen face now took turns in his mind with Lydia's bird-eaten face. He lay down, stretching over the backseat, feet dangling outside the open door. He thought he heard his phone buzzing somewhere in the front seat. He'll look in a second, he just needed to rest his eyes for a bit.

The morning sun heated up the car, and Dan woke with the brightness making him wish he was dead. His shirt soaked to the bone. He could feel sunburn on the tops of his feet. Almost getting sick when he sat up, Dan choked it back, and lit a cigarette. He fished around in the front seat until he found his phone. He had eight missed calls from Annie, but no voicemails, just a string of texts asking him what happened and why he wasn't picking up. Most of them were hoping he was okay and telling him he needed to call her. She was worried.

Annie walked through the diner carrying a tray overflowing with plates on her shoulder. She brought food to the booth at the back of the restaurant and passed Dan on her way back to the kitchen. She gave him a playful wink as he sat there stabbing his Bloody Mary with his celery. He added salt and pepper to it, took a sip, added more pepper, and stirred it again with the stalk. Annie sat across from him, holding a plate of food in one hand and the other tossing a rag over her shoulder. Dan picked at the food, both not hungry and starving. Annie picked up a slice of toast and dipped it in his egg, helping herself.

Dan didn't know what to say or where to begin. He never felt so defeated. "How'd it go last night?" he asked.

She shrugged, sidestepping. "Do you really want to get into it right now?"

"I guess, kind of."

"Well, I don't," she said. "What happened last night? I got so scared about that text, then you just disappeared."

Dan slid his phone face down across the table to Annie. She reached for it, but Dan grasped her hand, "It's shocking, you can't unsee it. Just...be prepared." Annie slowly turned the phone, hesitating, then, like a shot, she covered her mouth to smother her gasp. She quickly looked around, then at the phone again.

Annie gave the phone back to Dan and took his hand in hers, stroking his fingers with hers, lightly pinching them and not letting go.

"Dan, what are we going to do?"

He didn't feel great—drinking and smoking all night, the doom of Lydia's dead body, and the thought of Annie and her husband. Dan didn't know what to think anymore. He spent most of the night wanting to disappear into the darkness and fade from everyone's life for good. But hearing her say *we* again helped give him some comfort. Thinking of them together as a team, or whatever they might be. He was less sure now than ever, but she still saw them together in some way and, right now, he'd take any win he could.

"I have to tell him, I just don't—" He never finished

his thought, he simply held her hand and shrugged. He tried to drink, but his hand wasn't cooperating, unable to close around the glass. Annie let go of his good hand so he could drink. He swapped it with the bad one and let the alcohol calm his nerves and help him think straight.

Annie said, "Tell him here, maybe." Someone from the back of the diner called to her, *Miss!* and held up an empty soda glass, the ice mostly melted. Annie got up and wiped her hands on her apron.

"I'm not sure if that's a good idea," he said.

"Just think about it, at least. He's less likely to do something in a public place, I bet."

"I don't think he'd care."

"Less likely is still worth a shot." She ran the rag from her shoulder across the table and took Dan's empty glass. "I'll bring another one," she said and headed to the back of the restaurant to get the man's refill. When she brought Dan his second Bloody Mary, she told him she'd stop by his place after her shift so they could figure out what to do next.

9

DAN STILL HAD NO IDEA WHAT HAPPENED with Annie and her husband when she left that night, but now she was on top of him and working her hips back and forth real fast, moaning louder with each thrust, her sweat-slicked hair hanging over her face dripping beads of perspiration onto Dan's chest. She started trembling, her thighs tight around his hips, and he followed closely behind. She kissed him, clammy and quivering, then slid off him and lay with her back pressed to his chest, both exhausted and covered in each other's sweat, moaning with out-of-breath noises, fulfilled and more relaxed. Annie got up slowly and walked to the bathroom with her hand cupped between her legs. Dan lay on his back looking up at the ceiling. He was happy, and he wasn't. He never had problems with one-night stands or random hook-ups, but this was different.

Dan had to fight the urge to talk to Annie about what they were and what she was going through. He hoped they might have a future together, but knew they didn't. Did he have much of a future himself? Why not simply be happy and enjoy this for what it was? Enjoy her. Whatever he was to her didn't mean she couldn't be more to him. He tried to chase all those thoughts from his mind because even ideas like that were too much to focus on and risked ruining all the other things he felt. So he watched the sunlight as it bounced off the glass of the cars outside, peeking through his window from the crack in the curtains, and dancing along the ceiling. He heard the toilet flush and the sink run, and Annie walked over to him, not sexy, just normal, naked and beautiful. Comfortable, as if they had been together for years. Perfect with the dimples that ran along her thighs and dented the cheeks of her ass, the few days' growth of hair between her legs, and the extra bit of fat in her stomach below her belly button, her hips making a wide curve at her sides. He must have been smiling too much because she turned red, and hurried back to the bed, diving under the covers. She pulled them under her arms, tucked to her chin, and rolled closer to Dan, resting her head on his chest.

"You're so sweaty," she said and wiped her hand over him, then the blanket before laying her head again. He laughed and told her it was her fault, and she pinched his side. They embraced the silence, as her eyelashes fluttered over his skin like a butterfly wings. He felt them blink and stay closed. "What do you think happened to that girl from the church? Do you think she survived?"

"I'm not sure," he said. "I didn't see anyone doing anything more than pray. I hope she's okay."

He felt her cheek move as if to say something else, breathing in then holding it as if she changed her mind.

"What's up?"

With a solemn voice Annie asked, "How do you think Lydia died?"

"I couldn't tell when I saw her, and the pictures don't show anything. And the animals—"

"Do you think she did it to herself, maybe? Pills or a razor or something? I don't know what I hope for more. I'm not sure any way is better than the other. It makes me sad, though, you know, to think of someone doing that to her." She sat up against the headboard, sheets still tucked under her arms. "When do you think you're gonna tell Jackie?"

"That's what I've been trying to figure out. If he responds bad, like *bad* bad, and does something, and I rushed to tell him, I'd be cutting my own life even shorter."

"But maybe this would end it, and you'd be free. Wouldn't you want that sooner rather than later?"

"What happens then?" he asked.

"Whatever you want! Your life is yours again."

"No, I mean—"

"Oh." She turned her face away from him, and her voice got quiet. "I don't know. I guess we'd have to figure that out then, too. It's—"

"Complicated," he said. "I know."

"Don't say it like that. We haven't had time to sort anything out. If I didn't mean it, I wouldn't be here. I'm not that nice."

"Yes, you are."

"No, really," she turned to him, "I'm not. This is new to me. Once a cheater, always a cheater, but Dan, if that's true, I wouldn't know. It's my first time doing...*this*. Maybe I should be thinking about it more, but I can't bring myself to do it. I don't regret this, being with you, and I'm not ashamed of my feelings, but I don't exactly feel great about myself either. I never want to ruin the time with you by thinking."

"Or talking."

"That too. We'll have a bridge to cross soon enough, and we will. We'll cross it. Together. But until then, we have to get this *other* mess sorted out."

"Okay," he reached out for her hand, but she pulled her hand away.

"Not right now. I'm annoyed at you."

"Annoyed?"

"Maybe that's not the right word. I'm hurt, I guess, I dunno. What more do you need, Dan? I'm upset, so just let me sit here—never mind, I'm going outside for a cigarette."

She got up from the bed, taking the sheet with her, wrapped completely. She picked her clothes off the ground on the way and closed herself in the bathroom, and Dan heard the lock click. He ran his palms over his eyes as if it would jumpstart his thinking and he'd be able to navigate all of it, but it just made pink dots float in his vision like sparks popping from a fireplace, speckled in the smoke.

When Annie came out of the bathroom she was fully clothed and tossed the sheet on the bed. She was able to make enough space between the dresser and the broken door to squeeze out. He heard the spark of her lighter, and the smell of her cigarette drifted into the room. He wished he were out there with her. He messed his hair scratching at his scalp, massaging his hairline, which was tingling with embarrassment. He reached over and picked his phone off the nightstand and texted Jackie to meet at the diner tonight at nine o'clock.

Jackie's two goons entered first, and stood on each side of the door with their arms crossed low in front of their waists. Annie sat at the back of the diner in a booth as if she was dining alone. It was Dan's idea. He preferred her not come at all, but she insisted, so this was their compromise. Dan sat facing the door, sipping from his glass. He wanted no surprises. The diner was empty except for a couple who came in a few minutes after Dan and chose to sit right behind him. The taller of the goons, with the eyebrows, looked at Dan and smiled a real shit-eating grin. Fat Jackie came in wearing an all-white suit with a dark trench coat draped over his shoulders, resting like a cape. Christ, he was even wearing a fedora.

Jackie walked up to the booth out of breath, snorting and wheezing. The booth shook when he sat down, and the vinyl seat crinkled and squeaked under his weight. He took off his hat and placed it on the table, resting on the edge of the booth.

"What's this?" Jackie said and dipped his pinky into Dan's drink, and sucked his finger with a slurp. His face soured. "Is that pineapple vodka? You drink too much, kid. Anyone ever tell you that?"

"Yeah, my last sponsor. Jackie, look I—"

Jackie turned to his two henchmen. "There he goes again, Dan A-Plenty with his jokes. Your face looks like it's healing up okay. How's the hand?" He was grinning as he said it, taunting with his smile.

"Stiff and hurts like hell." Dan took a deep breath. "Jackie, I called you here—"

"You texted."

"I asked you to meet me here, because I have a development on—" he thought a moment, not knowing what to say. It wasn't a case because he wasn't a detective. "A development with the task you sent me on."

"A task you set yourself on," Jackie said. "By losing my money."

"Enough with the fucking commentary. I have news and you're not going to like it."

Every trace of power Jackie had over Dan left.

"What did you find out?" Jackie asked, all facades down, only fear and anxiety were left. It flooded his face. "Dan, is she okay?" He spoke like a friend, which knocked Dan off balance. The tone of a childhood spent together.

Dan rubbed his palm over his sweaty forehead. His hand trembled, and chills ran down his body. He almost chewed right through his bottom lip as he nervously pinched it between his teeth.

"Say something, goddamn it!" Jackie said, slapping on the table, making the silverware rattle, spilling some of Dan's drink.

Dan flinched. "Jackie, she's dead, I'm sorry."

"You're sor—What are you saying? What are you telling—You're sorry? How? When did you find out?"

"I found out last night."

"Last night!" He hit the table again, this time with his fists. "And you're only telling me now?"

Dan jumped again and timidly looked around. The waitress behind the counter stopped moving altogether.

Perfectly still, paused mid-cleaning of a glass and stood there with the dish rag half hanging from the cup like dirty grey milk, frozen as it spilled out. "Okay, man," Dan said, "try and stay calm. This is a public pla—"

Jackie smashed the table with both fists. "A public, do you think I give a fuck where we are, Dan? With what you just told me, do you think I—you want me to, to stay calm? Just because we're in some fucking shit-hole diner? That I am, what, not going to get upset that my fuck—that my daughter is—? I don't give—" All words stopped. He got up mid-sentence, his jacket falling to the ground. He turned to the booth behind them, looming tall and fat over the man sitting there. The man looked up at Jackie and went to say something, Jackie grabbed the man by the hair and lifted him to his feet. The man pulled at Jackie's fist but couldn't shake himself loose. The woman in the booth screamed. Jackie punched the man in the face. A wet smack rang out, then the guy's knees went loose like jelly, but he remained standing.

Another wet smack. "I." *Smack*. "Don't." *Smack*. "Fucking." He went to hit him again, but the man could no longer stay on his feet and fell. Jackie swung and missed. "Care."

Jackie left the man on the ground and turned to Dan, leaning over the table, resting on his fists, bloody and leaving knuckle marks on the Formica tabletop. Eyebrows went to the couple and threw a few hundred-dollar bills at them. Jackie's breath wheezed. The waitresses were screaming. The woman crying in hysterics, knelt next to the man on the floor, bleeding from his face. Dan looked past them to the back of the diner where Annie sat, her eyes wide as she watched the whole thing unfold, her hand covering her mouth. Dan looked back up at Jackie. His breath was calmer, but his face was shiny with sweat, his cheeks bright red.

"I don't care about you or any of these people, Dan. I'll burn this whole fucking town to the ground, and nothing will come of it. And the fucking Police Chief will STILL INVITE ME TO HIS DAUGHTER'S SWEET SIXTEEN. HOW DO YOU—how do you know she's..." Jackie got too choked up to finish.

"I saw her body, Jack." Dan looked straight ahead at nothing but a spot on the wall at the back of the place, too scared to make eye contact. Dan put his phone face down on the table. "There is a photo on this phone, but if you want to know the truth of it, I wouldn't look."

Jackie snatched the phone from the table and flipped it over, his face glowing from underneath with blue light. He gasped and immediately started sobbing. He put his head down and began to moan. A deep, gravely wail that started at the pit of his stomach and rolled up his gut and throat and out through his clenched teeth. He dropped the phone and rested his hands on the table, his head down and shoulders shaking. He put his hand on Dan's shoulder and mumbled something Dan couldn't hear. He asked him to repeat himself, and Jackie's head snapped up, the tears shining wet and sloppy on his face and in the fat wrinkles around his eyes.

"Where is she?" He looked over his shoulder out the window to the parking lot.

"There is this trail up in the hills near T-or-C."

"What are you saying? You just, you, you left my little girl there? Like that!"

"What did you want me to do? You asked me to find her. I'm sorry it turned out this way. I wish it was a better outcome—"

"You go get her and bring her back to me," he said through his teeth.

"No, Jack. I found her, I'll show you where she is, but I'm not going to do that. No. Have these assholes go get her."

When he turned to look at the two goons by the door, he saw Jackie move quickly out the corner of his eye. He heard a loud thud and a rattling of forks and knives, then a white-hot pain blistered through Dan's broken hand, sending fire up his arm. The pain was so intense he couldn't scream, he could only inhale gasps. Jackie smashed the metal napkin dispenser on his hand and pinned it under his heavy weight.

Finally, the scream escaped Dan's mouth. "GET OFF ME YOU FAT FUCK!" Spit flying and the f's sliding together as the saliva flooded his mouth.

In the next moment, Dan's head was smashed against the cold tabletop, but he didn't feel any pain from it. One minute he was screaming in pain, and the next his forehead was wet on the table with Jackie's hand pinning it down. Cool metal pressed to the side of Dan's temple. He heard the hammer click and felt the gun barrel twitch as it locked into place. Stuck, he watched the two goons pull their guns—one pointed to the waitresses behind the counter, screaming at them to stay still and drop the phone, the other with his gun towards the back of the diner where Annie was, telling her to sit back down. Jackie pressed the barrel harder into Dan face.

"You bring her back to me, or I will finish what we

started. I will collect your debt from everyone you love in any way I can think of. Do you understand? Your family, your friends." Jackie took Dan's phone off the table and put it in his pocket. "Anyone you've called or texted, I will track down and collect from them, too. Do you understand me? Bring me my daughter tomorrow."

He snapped his fingers at one of his goons and curled his fingers, *give-it-to-me*, and the guy reached into his pocket and tossed Jackie his cellphone. Jackie put it on the table.

"You can get in touch with me on that. I'm keeping yours." He pressed on the barrel again and the he pressure made Dan feel like his eyes might burst from his head. "Tomorrow." He finally let up. Jackie took out his own phone and pressed the screen. He began sobbing into the receiver. "Hun—no, I'm not." The conversation faded as the doors closed behind him. The shorter thug picked Jackie's coat off the ground, and Eyebrows grabbed his fedora and followed Fat Jackie outside.

The diner was still and quiet until they heard all three car doors slam and the gravel crunch under their tires. Dan sat up and saw the puddle of blood on the table. He clumsily picked some napkins from the dispenser with his one hand and held them to his brow. Annie was kneeling next to the woman on the ground, helping her lift the man back onto the bench in the booth so he was sitting up. He leaned his head back on the booth and closed his eyes.

"Don't let him fall asleep," Dan said, still pressing the napkins to his face. "In case he has a concussion."

"Janey, call an ambulance," Annie said. One of the waitresses picked up the phone, her hands trembling.

Annie sat beside Dan in the booth and took his head in her hands, turning it to the side and peeking under the napkins. She grimaced and pressed them hard into his face again. She gently picked up his broken hand, swollen and mangled. She tried to hold back her tears, but it wasn't working. "I'll go get the first-aid kit," was all she could manage.

In the bathroom again with Annie, leaning on the metal sink with her delicate hands going to work with the iodine and butterfly bandage and gauze.

She asked, "Are you really going to get the body?"

"I'm not sure if I have a choice. You saw what he is like. He's insane."

"Was he always like this?"

"Always an asshole, but this is something else. He's dangerous," Dan said. "In high school, maybe he'd push you into a locker. Smack you around in the bathroom, fuck up your car. Asshole shit. Jock shit. Nothing like this. I can handle that. If he were like this—I'd never have gone back to him for money." Dan lowered his voice, all anger and panic gone. His tone was as serious as she'd ever heard him. "Annie, really, I wouldn't have."

Annie crooked her mouth and said nothing, letting the statement hang between them. She nodded. "So, we get the body, then what happens?"

"No, I already dragged you too far into this. I can't have you do this, too. Tonight was the end of it." She placed the bandage over his eyes and pressed hard with her thumb. *"Ow, fuck!"*

"Stop saying things like that," she said. "So, what happens when we get the body?"

"I don't know."

"Is he ever going to let you go?"

"Every time I see him, it gets worse." His frustration grunted through his teeth. "It always fucking escalates. Every *fucking goddamn fucking* time!" His yell bounced around the steel of the bathroom. "But what can I do? I'm backed into a corner. You're in my phone, Annie. All of my recent texts and calls are with you. He has that now."

She closed up the first-aid kit. "Okay, I guess we'd better do this then." She grabbed his hand gently, and he winced. "This looks bad, Dan. We need to do something about it."

"Probably do now. It was starting to feel better." The swelling of his hand looked like something out of a cartoon, the skin so puffed that his knuckles became tiny indents that sliced his skin.

"We're going to need some stuff if we're doing this. Everything is closed, we'll go first thing in the morning."

Hearing that was a relief. After all that happened, he just wanted to lie in bed with Annie, passing a beer back and forth, watching the first movie they stumbled across on the TV, commercials and all. He didn't need any funny business, just her company. It's all he wanted. Not her going home and having those moments with her husband. Everything hurt. Every nerve and inch of his body was screaming. Dan didn't know if he could have taken her leaving on top of that.

It was darker than night, and no stars shone. Dan walked, stumbling through the darkness with his arm in flames and a coldness in his chest. He looked for

Annie—she wasn't there, but the birds were. They flew overhead, vomiting up rotten meat as they circled over Dan, splashing around him, crashing into divots, and tossing dust. Dan was shivering. He was alone. He thought he could smell Annie's shampoo, wafting around his face, pleasant at first, then gone altogether. A strange thud sounded in the dark. A shuffle, then another thud. It was close, whatever it was. Jackie. Did he take Annie?

Thud.

Shuffle.

Thud.

Dan woke with a jump, grunting as he flinched. He was alone in bed, and Annie's side was cold. Panicked, he scurried to the bedside table and flipped on the light. Annie was sitting by the open door, fully dressed, with her face glowing blue from her phone.

"Are you leaving?" Dan said. His brain still foggy from sleep, and for a moment, he didn't know if he was still in his dream.

"Did you have another nightmare?" Annie placed her phone face down on her lap.

"Yeah. Are you leaving?"

"Yeah," she said. Her voice was weak, and she was sniffling.

"Give me a second to put something on, I'll give you a ride. We'll talk on the way." Dan sat up and took a deep breath, digging his feet into the carpet.

"I already called an Uber." She checked her phone. "It's fifteen minutes away."

"Oh." Dan felt punched in the gut. "You're *leaving* leaving."

"I'm sorry," Annie started, but Dan put his hand up,

telling her she didn't need to say it. He was surprised at how much he meant it. He was still groggy and knew the sting of what was happening was dulled by sleep—but Annie owed him nothing. He couldn't ignore the panic vibrating around in his stomach at the thought of her not being around, but in this moment, he understood. The pain searing through his arm and face made it hard to hold anything against her. How could he expect anyone to put themselves through this for him? He didn't know if he could get mad at her, maybe in time, if he had enough time left. "I'm scared, Dan," she said. "I am beside myself. That's Jackie? He's—"

"Crazy."

"It's more than that, but I don't know what." She took a deep breath. "I just want to go back to my normal life." Her words poured out in a mixture of sobs and anxiety. "And I *hate* it. I hate that life, *so, so much*. I didn't know. You warned me, and I...I don't know, I believed you, I thought I did."

"Annie, it's okay. You've already done so much—"

"And I want you, Dan. You. No one else. You have this way of looking at me that...it just cuts right through me. Even before all of this. At work, I have to be a certain type of way. I have to be *on*. For business, for tips. Then I go home, and, and...I have to be *on* again. It's different. With Trevor, I'm so uncomfortable now. He's more of a stranger than the people I wait on. I don't know how to be around him, and it's exhausting. Dan, I don't even laugh around him. It's not about happiness, it's about, just how *embarrassing* and...and *vulnerable* laughing feels around him. I don't want to show him that. Maybe it's resentment, but I don't want him to see any flaws. But, *ugh*, that sounds...it's not like that. I want him to only see a statue. Or the slab that hides the statue. Everything feels like *work*. I don't have to be on with you. And that's *so* nice. But we have *this*." She buried her head in her hands. "I don't know which is worse."

Dan walked to where she was sitting and rubbed her back.

"Do you hate me?" she asked softly.

"Not at all. I'll miss you, though. Annie, I get it. I'll be okay."

"Really?"

"Probably not, but I can't ask you to stay. I know how Jackie is, and if something happened to you—I'd rather you leave. I can't have you get hurt. Not for me."

"I don't want to leave you."

"I know."

"He doesn't know about me. You get it, right?" Dan didn't say anything back. It was true, she was clear of it. No one knew she existed, only Dan. Jackie wouldn't even think to look for her. At most she's just a number in his phone. Maybe Dan could convince her to leave altogether. Leave him, leave Trevor. Not tell him where, just go and leave no trace. Before he could say anything, Annie sat up straight and checked her phone. The map showed the driver was five minutes away. Annie canceled the car.

Dan's hand came to a stop along her back as he tried to make sense of it.

"If he doesn't know about me, and if we can keep it this way, then I don't have to leave. I can stay with you. The faster we get this done, the quicker you're free, and we're free. And this is all behind us. It'll be easier with the two of us."

"I can't ask you to stay. You brought up a lot of good points."

"Including this one," she said and closed the door. "Help me move the dresser."

"Are you sure?"

She smiled, resolved. Then she kissed him.

"No," she said. "But more than I was. Hearing it out loud helped. I can't have you fending off your nightmares alone. Grab the other end."

And the two of them blocked the door and crawled back into bed, Annie settling into the nook of Dan's arms, warming his chest. She fell asleep before he did, and when he finally did, he dreamt of fishing.

10

"WHAT DO YOU THINK OF THIS?" ANNIE whispered, looking over her shoulder down the aisle of the department store to make sure no one was within earshot. She was holding an over-sized rubber tub and a lid.

"We can't bring Jackie his daugh—" he lowered his voice. "His daughter in a goddamn Rubbermaid container like she's unused Christmas decorations." Tired and frustrated, Dan dug the palms of his hands into his eyes, wincing at the pain that ran up his arm. "Fuck, this is fucking nuts, you know that, right?" He pulled at his hair. "What did I get you into? I should have let you leave."

Annie just looked at him, her eyes welling up. She rolled them back and blinked a few times. Her voice came out in a broken whisper. "You keep thinking. I'm going to find something for your hand."

When Dan returned to the car, Annie was already waiting with the A/C on. They did their transactions at separate times to avoid any suspicion. She got the large rubber storage tub, garbage bags, and two sets of dish gloves. Dan got a large canvas duffel bag, a brace for his hand, some air freshener trees, and one that went in the air vents of the dashboard. The car was cool and smelled of cigarettes and the motel shampoo Annie had to use. Dan didn't like getting rid of that scent, but he knew how bad this would get, so he plugged the air freshener into the vent and tossed everything else in the back. Annie asked to see his hand and slowly slid the brace over his knuckles, sticking his thumb through the hole, and they pulled the Velcro as tight as he could stand and then tugged it tighter before closing it. It didn't do much for the pain, but hopefully in time it would. Annie put a cigarette in his mouth and lit it for him before doing the same for herself.

"Oh," she reached into the plastic bag between her feet on the floor. "I also got this." She held up a small rubber object that looked like a bright yellow pill with a seam in the middle. "It's a snake bite kit. After you told me about that church, I got the heebie-jeebies." She let out a cartoonish shiver down her spine and shook it out of her face, her cheeks rippling from side to side. "I meant to grab some antivenom from work. I think they have an emergency stash for," she laughed, "for emergencies. But with all the chaos last night—I think this should work in a pinch." She tossed the kit into the glove compartment, took a deep breath, and sighed. "Are we ready?"

"As I'll ever be." He checked the dashboard. "I have to get gas."

"I'll get us some snacks."

Dan backed out of the spot and headed down the road, wavy in the heat.

Annie's snacks were significantly better than Dan's were. No eggs or jerky. Instead, she got them each a buttered roll and a bag of pretzels, two packs of cigarettes, and two tallboys each for the road. The trip started quietly enough, asking him how he felt and how his hand was, or asking if he needed her to drive. They talked about the landscape and the lizards that ran across the road. She commented on how many dust devils she was seeing, one of them hitting the side of the car with a thump, like a ram charging into the driver's side door. They sang along with the songs on the radio and smoked their cigarettes. Dan was happy, all things considered, and on some stretches of road, he even forgot what they were about to do. But then it would creep in again in the silence between songs, and he'd feel Jackie's grasp on his soul and knew he'd never let go.

Delivering Lydia wouldn't be enough, there would be something else, and then something else, and another thing after that. He felt trapped now, and the car felt small, like there was no air, and he rolled down the window so he could breathe. His hairline started to leak and spread out its needles across his scalp and along the back of his head like a crown. All of this over ten thousand dollars. Maybe that's too much money to let Dan off the hook, but all of this? Threatening his family and people in his phone? It was bullshit, and it was now the entirety of his life, forever—odd jobs and getting smacked around by Jackie while his two goons piss themselves with laughter. Dan let out a grunt and smacked the steering wheel so suddenly that it made Annie jump, then the pain flooded his body.

"What's wrong?" she asked.

"Annie, what are we even doing? This is never going to stop, I know it. I know him, I know this *fucking* guy. I told you back that first day, in the bathroom, I told you he was just fucking with me. All of this, this endless fucking goose chase. You don't think he has people to do this? Of course he does, so why me? Why the guy that can't win. Why the guy who makes these terrible decisions? Why the guy with a drinking problem? Why not someone reliable he can trust? I'm on the hook. Forever. Each thing I do won't be good enough. It's probably how he got all of his guys working for him. Some fucking Stockholm Syndrome shit. It's never going to end. I'd be better off letting him blow my goddamn fucking brains out the back of my skull."

"You don't mean that."

"Honestly, I do. I should let him do that, put me out of my misery. He should have done it last night! Everything hurts, I'm running all over God's creation jumping through fucking hoops, and then what? I do this, and it all repeats? I should just have him do it and save me the trouble of doing it myself." Dan's face was red and hot, and he stared ahead at the endless stretch of road that disappeared into a point, his jaw clenched. Annie was quiet, and it took him a while before he snapped out of it and heard the soft sniffle from the passenger seat. He looked over at Annie, and the tears streaming down her cheek, running her palm across her face, continuing to look out the window. Her body was turned away from him. Dan tried to remove the annoyance from his voice, but he wasn't sure if he did.

"Why are you crying?"

Annie ran her fingers under her eyes again and stared out the window until his question was gone and nothing was left except the static rattling out of the radio when the music faded in and out.

"Why do you think I'm crying, Dan? I'm sorry things are going this way for you, and you're hurting so much. I hate it. Seeing you like this. *I'm trying,* Dan. I know this all has nothing to do with me, but I care." She sighed. "And I'm trying everything I can think of. Everything. What I'm going through at home. That's on me, I get it. But," more exhaustion weighed on her voice. "You say you make all these terrible decisions, but you chose me, and I chose you. Is that terrible? Aside from all of this, has that been a horrible decision? Know what, don't answer that because I'm sure it'll just hurt. I don't know how many times I have to tell you that I care for you and that I don't regret anything. I feel like it's all I talk about. And then you go on these...these...*fucking rants* where you wish for death *every two seconds* or say you're going to kill yourself. What do you want me to do with that? What am I supposed to say?"

Her voice was calm and didn't shake, and her chin didn't quiver, but tears still rolled down her cheeks as she spoke. Dan tried to look at her, but she kept her gaze out the window, so he focused back on the road and corrected the car back to his lane.

"I don't know what happens after this," she said. "And I don't know what Jackie will do, and I don't know what Jackie won't do. But I'm sure of what he'll do if we don't bring Lydia back to him, and since that's the *only* thing we do know, we should do it. Because if we don't, then you're—" A tear rolled down her cheek and hung off the bottom of her chin. Hanging but not falling until she ran her fingertips along her jawline and collected it. "And, no, I don't know what happens if we get through this, I haven't allowed myself to think about it. I'm too scared to think that far ahead."

Annie turned from the window and looked out the windshield, resting on the headrest, and put a cigarette between her lips. She cracked the window, and the loudness of the wind completely drowned out the radio. All the effort she used to keep her voice from trembling showed itself as the quivering worked its way down her neck and across her chest, down her arms, where it came out of her hands—the lighter shaking as she sparked it.

She blew the smoke out of her nose and a stream from her mouth, becoming one. "Just keep driving," she said. "That's what I want to say. Just keep going. We'll find a new town and a new state, and a new motel with a door that works. And we'll drink and dance and screw. And you'll heal, and this would be some memory, and we'll wonder if it was all a dream." She let out a deep, slow breath.

"I'm okay with that, though," he said. "Annie, I'll do it. I'll just keep driving. I'm serious."

"I know you are," her voice airy and defeated. "And I am too. But what about everyone else? We can't do that to them."

"I don't know, maybe we can? Maybe it's a bluff. Maybe it's all him fucking with me. Another way for him to keep the screws in. Maybe we call his bluff and just keep going."

"Are you really willing to risk it?"

Dan punched the wheel with his palms and let out a groan. He gripped tight, took a deep breath, and screamed "FUCK!" as loud as he could. Annie jumped, but then laughed, and shouted "FUCK!" And he laughed. Together, they both screamed it as loud as they could until their breath ran out, and they both began coughing. They laughed until tears of laughter replaced the tears from before, and they both sat lower in their seats, winded and spent. Annie reached between her legs into the plastic bag and handed him a beer. He popped it open with his finger and took some swigs, keeping it low below the dashboard and out of sight. Annie rested her beer on her knee and looked out the window.

"If I make it through this in one piece, like really get through to the other side," he looked at her, and she turned to him. "We'll do it. We'll just get in the car and drive, start somewhere new where no one knows us, and we know no one. Reverse Cheers, we'll go where nobody knows our name."

She held her gaze on him, lips curling into a crooked smile.

"Okay," she said.

The timing was going to be the hard part, and Dan knew that. It was stuck in his head for most of the drive, and he made sure not to open his second beer to keep his mind clear and his head on straight. They needed enough of the evening darkness to keep from being seen when they got her, but enough time left for the drive back to Jackie. Dan had no idea how literal he was when he said tomorrow, but he didn't want to find out. It was seven o'clock when they got there, still some dying redness to the sky. If they waited an hour, and were able to get in and out quickly enough, they could make it back to Jackie by eleven. It was cutting it close, but they couldn't risk it.

Annie sat on the hood of the car, and Dan leaned back against it, one foot on the bumper, nervously smoking a cigarette back-to-back, camel humping the new one with the old one. He started to feel a little sick from smoking and drinking, but maybe it was just the thought of what they came here to do. Annie watched him smoke, seeing his nervous energy in his shoulders and hands, even though he tried to hide it.

"It really is beautiful up here," she said. "I can see why she loved it." She dropped the butt onto the dirt below. "It's very romantic, this view and this sky. Don't you think?"

"Yeah, except for why we're here."

"It's still a romantic atmosphere, if you take away the specifics."

He dropped his cigarette, too, and crushed it under his foot, confused by the electric charge between them. "Are you trying to go into the backseat like teenagers?"

"It could be a good way to kill an hour," she said, a devilish smile crossing her face.

"Don't threaten me with a good time." He watched her hop off the car and wipe the dust caked on the hood from the drive from her backside. She nudged her head to the backseat, and Dan shrugged, following her with a grin. She sat in the back, pushing their supplies to the floor, and slid across the seat until she was resting on the hard plastic of the door. Dan crawled in after her, awkwardly lying between her legs. He reached behind and tried to close the door, but it hit against his back. They scrunched more so he could get it closed. They started giggling, and she lifted her leg clumsily over his head until she wasn't lying down anymore. Dan leaned over the small bump of the center seat and cradled her chin. He turned her face to him and kissed her, tasting the beer and nicotine from her tongue. He placed a hand on the outside of her shirt, lightly cupping her breast, and moved his body closer, bumping his head on the ceiling. Their laughter filled the car.

Dan sat forward and leaned back, arching his ass off the seat, unbuttoning his jeans, and unzipping his fly. Annie lifted his shirt and tried to pull his jeans and briefs down, tugging, but his knees hit the seat in front of him. "I need a bigger car," he joked, wiggling his jeans under his thighs. Annie kissed his neck and worked her hand down to his crotch, moving it over him. Pumping slowly, trying to get a reaction, but no blood flowed. She kissed his neck and behind his ear, but still nothing. He rolled his body toward her and kissed her neck and rubbed her through the crotch of her jeans, but he still got no movement. He buried his face in her neck and stopped kissing. He let out a defeated chuckle.

"This isn't working, sorry. I am just, I don't know. Too much going on right now, I guess?"

"I wasn't in the mood either." She cradled his face with her hand. "Figured it was worth a shot. Try and take our minds off things." She lowered his shirt.

Dan kissed her long and sweet on her lips. He

sat with his pants down, looking at his softness as it leaned over the side of his crotch. "I'm not sure if that ever happened to me before. I probably should be embarrassed."

"You going to pull those up?"

He fixed his pants and squeezed his upper body between the seats to turn the car on. The radio came back to life, some static, but the music was clear enough. Dan watched the clock as they listened to the music, looking out the windshield at the view with Annie resting her head on his shoulder, slipping her fingers between his and squeezing his hand tightly.

It was a little before eight when it was dark enough to start their task. They grabbed the duffel bag and lined it with the garbage bags. They tossed the gloves in, zipped it up, then placed everything into the rubber tub, and headed out to the wilderness.

11

DAN TRIED TO PREPARE ANNIE FOR THE smell. That ungodly scent of death and rot. But he knew no matter what he said, nothing could prepare her for what she was about to encounter. The two walked along the dark trail carrying the tub holding the supplies they needed, each holding a handle. The night was dead quiet, except for the wind, and the dirt and rocks grinding under their feet. The stench swallowed them more with every step. Anxiety riddled Annie's face, her tears building but not falling. Then the dam finally broke and the stronger the smell, the more tears rolled down her cheeks. Dan wondered why they didn't grab some sort of face mask, but doubted it would've done much good. They covered their noses and mouths with their shirts, and Dan heard Annie stifling her retching, coughing it down. He followed suit the closer they got.

Then came the birds.

The whooshing of their large wings as the vultures

fought to maintain balance on Lydia's body in their twisted version of King of the Hill—hissing and grunting as they fought over the remaining morsels they would carve out. The sharp curve of their beaks disappeared before reemerging, dangling with skin and stringy muscle as they worked their necks to swallow the rotting gristle. Some flew off as the two approached with their container. Vomiting up chunks of Lydia to quicken their takeoff. But some birds stayed. Hungry and defiant, their glassy pupils glowing red in the hot spotlight of Annie's phone.

"Oh my God," she gasped.

Dan screamed as he ran at the remaining birds. "Goddamn monsters!" He kicked dirt and pebbles, the sand floating in the wind, hanging and swirling before falling back to the ground. He picked up rocks and hurled them at the vultures. More stones sailed past him as Annie did the same. The last one, the big one, standing on what was left of Lydia's chest, remained unflinching through the yelling and the barrage of rocks. Dan ran toward it, screaming, missing his kick by inches. Then the bird was gone, leaving only feathers arching back and forth falling peacefully in the quiet.

When Dan turned back, he saw that Annie had removed one of her gloves. She walked over to Lydia and went slowly to her knees, hand to her face. Dan didn't know what she was thinking, but it was more than shock or disgust. She tilted her head, tears streaming down her cheeks, her face contorted in heartbreak. She gently moved wisps of hair from Lydia's face, matted in blood, and tucked them behind what was left of her ear. She apologized and clasped the bones of Lydia's hand with her glove. Annie sat with her head down, then stood up and dabbed her eyes with the top of her wrists. She gave Dan a slow nod, and he removed the supplies from the tub.

Dan lined the tub with garbage bags, and did the same to the duffel, before placing it into the container. He gently placed the tub next to Annie and Lydia. The air around them was weird—it felt silly to think, but it was the only way Dan could put it. Weird. Thick with the horrors of what happened to Lydia, and the horrors of having to box her up. The wind amplified the calmness but nothing about this would be nice or delicate. Dan couldn't help but feel the need for some kind of gentleness, he couldn't just plop the tub down, kicking up dirt. He couldn't be mindless about this, he needed decorum, especially for Annie. He couldn't be all business, cold and disconnected. Nothing fit this situation. It was a funeral and a crime scene. A church in a viper's den. Dan ran the back of his wrist over his running nose.

Anne broke the silence, "How old do you think she is?"

"I'm not sure. Young. Jackie is a few years older than me, so maybe twenty-two, twenty-three. Depending on how quickly after high school he had her."

Annie made no attempt to wipe the tears from her cheeks or chin, where they hung fighting gravity. "God, I remember being that age," Annie said. "Except I was already married. Newly married. Whole life ahead of you. You feel like you know everything, but part of you knows you know nothing. *Absolutely nothing*. So full of life. Trevor was full of life." She hesitated, but kept her gaze on Lydia. "Possibilities seemed endless. You think you'll be happy forever, but then you realize you're not happy. And you haven't been happy. You realize you're not free. You feel trapped," her voice turned to a whisper, almost quietly mumbling to herself. *"Just so impossibly trapped.* And you wish you could just disappear, even if it's only for a few days—just to go hiking in the desert—anything. To feel free. Even if it's just an illusion. I dream of just leaving, disappearing, no word to anyone. And the next time anyone heard from me, I'd be some place I've never been. Spain, maybe."

"Spain?"

"Or France. I don't know, some place foreign and unknown. I love the idea of walking down the street, a stranger to everyone. No expectations, no history. Truly free. That's why I got the job at the diner. My own money. I don't need to work. I couldn't handle being so, just so entirely...*dependent* on someone. Anyone. We were happy once, I guess."

Dan didn't know anything about Annie's husband. He never wanted to either. He supposed that he still didn't, but this felt different. He didn't mind it much right now. Annie was going through it. It's too much to process. He knew how that felt.

"What happened?" Dan asked before he realized anything came out of his mouth.

"Life," she paused. "Maybe? I don't know. We wanted kids at one point. I'm not sure if I did, but I think I did. I was pregnant, but it didn't last. It's not like the movies, it didn't break us—for a while, we were closer. Then it faded. Maybe some people just don't make sense together? We met in high school. But it got to a point where he was my whole life. Not in a romantic way. As long as I can remember, he was always there, and we were always together. My whole life. Maybe that wears on a person. We don't fight. We just don't talk. Roommates with a certificate. He's a good guy, I just, I don't know, Dan, I just get *so angry* when I see him. Inside. And that's not right. And that's not fair to him. I couldn't...I can't take it anymore. I get home from work and sit in my car, right in the driveway. I feel so broken in half."

Dan didn't know what to say, so he said nothing. They stood there in the dark, looking down at Lydia, bright in the glow of their lights. The wind hovered dust around them.

"Annie, I think we better get started. I'm sorry."

They picked up Lydia. Annie took her shoulders because Dan didn't want her to have to deal with the missing lower half—the hollow, empty ribcage and remaining entrails. Annie stabilized the body on the lip of the container, and Dan slid the plastic-lined duffel over his end before pulling it over Lydia's head. But as they lowered her into the tub, they couldn't. The shoulders and ribs were too broad. They lifted her again, and Dan tried his end first, turning the body to the side. Still, she didn't fit. They pulled Lydia out once more, and Annie tried lowering her headfirst, slowly and gently. But they were still unable to get her in.

"Shit," Dan said. Punctuating the night. He repeated the word over and over and over. Grimacing through his teeth, and punching at his head. "*God*-fucking-*damnit!*" He took a deep breath and tried to calm himself. "Annie, why don't you go over there."

"No, I want to help."

"I know." He took another deep breath, ignoring the smell. "It's—Annie, she's not going to fit like this."

"What do we do?"

"I—" He tried to steady his voice. "I have to make her fit. And I don't want you to be around for it."

"Dan."

"Annie, please!"

"Jackie will kill us if we do that to her."

"He won't know it was us. We don't have a choice. *Please.*"

The please came out with such exhaustion and defeat that Annie knew she wouldn't be able to get through to him anymore, so she walked off into the night with her feet illuminated by the light of her phone. When she was far enough, Dan turned to Lydia.

"I'm sorry. I'm sure you deserved better."

No matter what they did, the car reeked of death. No amount of air fresheners helped. They had trees hanging all over and clips in the A/C vents. They threw their shoes and clothes in the trunk with Lydia. The stench on their clothes was the only thing they didn't account for, and now they were stuck in their underwear, knowing there was no way of talking themselves out of trouble if they got stopped on the road. Annie sat in the passenger seat, staring at her hand. She rubbed her fingertips together against her thumb as if she were feeling the texture of some imaginary fabric. The odor worked its way through the gloves and was stuck on their skin forever.

"I don't think I'll ever get that sound out of my head," Dan said. He turned the car on, and they drove off into the darkness.

* * *

They hadn't said anything since they left the site. Even when they undressed and put everything into the trunk, they did it with an unspoken understanding. Dan kept his eyes on the road, occasionally glancing over whenever Annie was illuminated by a passing car or the moon, or a streetlamp hanging from a telephone pole. The light would pass over the hood, crawling along the dashboard, across her lap—her thighs dimpled and pale. The beams would continue over the small pouch that sat below her stomach and the tiny rolls that hung over her waistband, moving up her chest, before illuminating the glow of tears falling from her cheeks. Then she'd fade into the black again.

Dan couldn't get the smell out of his nose. It was so strong on his hands as if they didn't even wear gloves. When he was younger, Dan once helped his grandfather repair a roof, all hot, sticky, and gross. No matter what, the tar clung to his fingers, and under his nails, so his grandfather washed their hands with gasoline from the lawnmower to get them clean. It was the only thing Dan could think of that might help—and if it didn't, he'd rather smell of gas than a rotting body and vulture throw up.

The gas station where he had passed out two nights ago was glowing in the distance, and it was the only landmark Dan knew of besides the rattlesnake church. He pulled the car deep into the shadows. Annie asked what he was doing, the silence finally pierced, her voice tired and weak.

"I need to do something about this smell," he said. "And I'd like to get you some clothes if I can. Normally, I wouldn't mind, but now I feel guilty about it." He didn't know why he tried to make a joke.

"I'm fine, really," she said. "Please, we should keep going." She turned and looked out the back window to the endless blackness. "What if someone sees you?"

"I'll be quick, I don't think anyone would suspect anything. No one knows she exists."

"Dan."

"I didn't mean it like that. She's not on the news or anything. No one would have any reason to suspect anything. I'll just look like some drunk mess." Dan chuckled. "I'll be convincing." He took the can of beer from the cup holder and rattled it to see how much was left. He took the remaining few sips and swished them in his mouth like mouthwash, puffing his cheeks and alternating back and forth. He swallowed, then poured the last few drops that clung to the bottom of the can into his hand and rubbed his palms together, smacking his face like cologne.

The man behind the counter looked up and stared as Dan walked into the gas station in nothing but his underwear and a pair of sneakers with his hair messed up and greasy, reeking of beer, with his wallet in his hand, muttering to himself.

"Don't ask," Dan said, but the man still studied him. "Like I told you last time, if it wasn't for bad luck, I'd have none at all." Dan laughed at his own joke. "The old lady catches me with another woman, so what? Who's perfect?" Dan walked over to the end cap of one of the makeshift aisles and thumbed through the generic tie-dye shirts with the city's name across them. He couldn't imagine that they sold many of these in the middle of nowhere, but was glad they carried this touristy bullshit. Dan grabbed a set for him and Annie and placed them on the counter. He grabbed two more tall boys from the fridge and a large bottle of water, stacking them next to the clothes. "I mean, yes, the other woman *was* her sister, but still. All my clothes right into the goddamn pool. That ugly bitch. She had my car and didn't even fill up the tank, so now I ask you, who is the real villain here? I'm the one stranded in my underwear? She should be mad at her sister, not me! She was the sober one! Whatever, fuck the both of them. Do you sell gas cans? I'll need a few bucks worth to find a hotel."

"Don't sweat it, brother, we've all been there. Been. There." He reached down and placed a gas can on the counter along with another nip bottle. "Don't worry, I got you. Need anything else?"

A car hadn't passed in the last ten minutes by the time Dan returned in a tie-dyed shirt two sizes too big for him and sweatpants that stopped above his shins with a plastic bag in one hand and the gas can in the other. The sweats were a good fit for Annie. The shirt hung on her like a nightgown, but did its job. They stood behind the car on the passenger's side and poured gasoline from the can onto their palms, scrubbing them over each other. They did it one more time, then used the water to rinse off the gas. They smelled their fingers, and Annie needed one more pass. It wasn't great, but it was better. Dan dumped the rest of the gas into the tank and put the can in the trunk, hoping any residual gasoline smell might help cover the rest.

Dan popped the top off one of the beers with a hiss that rattled around the quiet car, and handed it to Annie, who sat with her hands pinched between her knees, looking at her feet. He nudged her arm, and she gave him a weak smile, and took the can.

"I got this too," Dan said, handing her the small bottle of Fireball. Annie shook her head, and Dan placed it in the cup holder between them. She nursed her beer, then grabbed the pack of cigarettes.

"Do you think we'd explode if I lit one?" she said.

"We washed ourselves off, so I don't think so? That might only happen in cartoons," he said. He picked up the water, holding the bottle at the ready. Annie flicked the lighter, her face scrunched with hesitation. The spark did nothing but turn into the flame that lit Annie's cigarette. She cracked her window, and the night air pulsed through the car as she extended her fingers slenderly to Dan, the butt pinched loosely between them. He leaned over and took a pull, keeping his eyes on the road—the high beams no match for the darkness looming in front of them.

The streets were empty when they got to Fat Jackie's neighborhood. Dan tried to remember where his building was. They were all familiar, and each road was identical to the last—abandoned warehouses, cloudy and broken windows. Annie chewing her fingernails to the quick, bouncing her leg anxiously on the ball of her foot. Dan left the neighborhood without realizing it and pulled a U-turn at the next intersection, approaching it from the other side, which was more recognizable.

The scene felt too low-key, almost boring. It felt off. Dan thought of the body in the trunk and the way she looked as he broke her apart. The pin-drop silence of the desert broken with the sounds of joints and sockets turning and grinding, and tearing. Piercing the quietness of the desert as loud as a tree snapping in the wind.

When Dan was younger and living on Long Island with his dad, before his mom got custody back, before he and Jackie ever crossed paths in the hallways or even lived in the same state, Dan slept in his dad's bed one hurricane season, hugging tightly to him as the wind howled. The lights flickered, then Dan heard that crack, deafening like a whip by his ear, before the ceiling caved in, water flooding the bed as a tree crashed through the side of the house. Dan would have been crushed if his dad hadn't rolled him away at the last second. That sound stayed with him ever since, waking him up some nights, flinching for his dad. The sound Lydia's body made out in the desert, her sternum cracking, took the place of those haunts and became his new nightmare. The stench and gristle, the skin hanging from her limbs, most of her gone.

Dan knew he'd be tormented by that forever, and he knew that the world would keep turning as if none of it ever happened. Quiet, empty roads, so still—no lights, not even a wet, rain-soaked street, nothing. Not a thing that showed the universe cared about any of it. About Annie, him, Lydia. Cold and silent indifference. Everyone's lives going on exactly the same as before. The thoughts were chased from his mind by the sharp echoing of Annie's door closing. The two of them stood by the trunk of the car, trying to gather the courage to see this through to the end, and how Jackie would respond to what was waiting for him inside this container.

"Stay here," said Dan. "And stay out of sight, like we said. He can't hurt you if you're just a name on a phone."

Dan started to open the trunk but stopped. He leaned over and lightly pinched Annie's chin between his thumb and index finger. He tipped her face to his, the gasoline strong on his hands, and kissed her. Soft and slow and sweet. Trying to say the things he didn't know how to say. Her eyes were closed, and so were his, lingering on her lips. It was the first kiss they've shared where they weren't stabbing each other with their tongues or biting at each other's lips. The moment hung sweetly in the air only for a moment before the smell of death wafted up from the trunk and intruded on their intimacy, reminding them that Fat Jackie was waiting for him.

"Nice outfit," Eyebrows said, turning to his partner. "You know what he looks like?"

"Yes, I do," the short one said.

"You look like a faggot."

"A faggot."

"And you smell like shit."

"Like shit."

"Very enlightening, thank you. Classy as always," Dan said, holding the bin, resting it on his thighs. The container wasn't light, but it wasn't as heavy as Dan figured it would be. The room was how he remembered it, strangely wet. He thought maybe he saw stains of his blood on the cement, but it was hard to tell with this dark, shitty lighting. The place echoed, and Dan noticed how loud his footsteps were in the hall, echoing around him and trailing down the hall. Last time he was here, his eardrums were stabbing through his brain, and everything hurt. He hated these two guys and their moronic laughter. “Shut the fuck up and get Jackie.”

The man with the eyebrows clenched his teeth, his jaw stabbing into his cheeks. He shot a sharp breath out of his nose, and tried to snatch the door open defiantly, but struggled, the metal scraping against itself, fighting to stay closed. He disappeared, and the short man stood staring at Dan with the rubber bin in his hands. The rust made the door open so loud and unexpectedly that Dan flinched, scurrying back a few steps, his feet grinding across the grit of the cement floor. He expected Jackie to come in with that fat smirk across his face and some snide comments about his outfit and him being a loser, but Jackie didn’t say anything. He came in somber and quiet with a handkerchief in his hand. Dan softly placed the container on the floor.

“Open it.”

“Jackie, I don’t think you should, not here.” He leaned his head toward Eyebrows, and the other guy. “Not in front of these assholes.”

“Open it,” Jackie said. Eyebrows tucked his hand across his chest and into his jacket, holding it there. Dan inhaled, long and slow to show his hesitation, but did what Jackie demanded. When the lid came off, the stench filled the room almost instantly, the goons coughing gags into their fists. Jackie covered his mouth and nose with his handkerchief, and he nodded to the duffel bag in the container. “Show me.”

“Come on, man.”

“Show. Me.”

Dan reached down and opened the bag, showing Jackie Lydia’s pale, rotting face—the eyes covered in white film, her teeth showing through her cheek, the half-eaten ear on the side of her face. The short man turned away, and Dan watched Eyebrows double over with his hands on his knees and vomit on the ground between his feet. Jackie's knees buckled slightly. Mixtures of coughs and sobs filled his handkerchief. Dan focused on the ceiling, doing everything he could to not look at Lydia.

"Okay, enough. Close it."

Dan closed the container and slid it over to Jackie. He stepped back and started for the door.

"I'm sorry for your loss, Jackie." The sentiment hung in the air, unanswered, mixing with the smell of death and the stench of Eyebrow's throw-up. Jackie stood sniffling into his fist, looking down at his daughter. He knelt down and placed his hand on the lid. Dan was invisible. "I'm done here." He grabbed the cold metal handle of the door, textured with rust that was repeatedly painted over for years.

Jackie broke the silence of the room, his voice croaking, "Who would do this?"

Dan should have kept it rhetorical. He should have let it linger in the air unanswered, just like his condolences. Let Jackie ask his two stupid goons. That's what Dan should have done.

But instead, he answered.

"I'm not sure, Jackie. It's horrible, I can't imagine what—"

"Find them."

"I hope you do, man, I really do. Get some answers. Some closure."

"Find them. Find who did this to my little girl."

"No," Dan said, dread crawling through the pit of his stomach, face flushed and tingling with pinpricks. "Jackie, no. Come on. I found her. That's the extent of my abilities. Look at me. I'm a wreck. I mean it. I'm just some drunken asshole who is shit with money. This is beyond me."

"Shut up." Jackie snapped his fingers at his two goons, curling his fingers in a quick motion. Eyebrows reached into his coat pocket, threw Jackie Dan's phone, then left the room. Jackie pressed the screen, a pale blue light glowing under his face.

"How did you unlock—"

Jackie started scrolling through his phone, "Who is... *Annie Diner?* You talk to her a lot. Calls, and...and a lot of texts. You guys seem to be an item," Jackie continued to scroll and read, his eyes still wet, sniffling, a mixture of his emotions runny in his nose. "It seems to be very new." He held up the phone to face Dan, showing a string of texts. "However, you seemed to have dragged her into this."

"She's not part of it, leave her out of it."

"No, Dan, she *is* part of it, and it's all your doing. Because that is what the fucking destructive black hole of your existence does, Dan. It pulls people in, and you rub off on them. So, now she's involved, and if you don't do this, Dan, then I'll kill you. I'll kill you and get my money from her. Or maybe I'll just kill her and get my money from you still." Jackie's face was trembling. "That's *why you,* Dan, because your stink is already all over this. You and your bad fucking luck. You ruin everything you touch. You always have. This is already stained with your fucking stench. Do you get what I'm saying, Dan? Do you? Maybe you'll actually have some good luck, and all of your bad luck will rub off on whoever did this. You can turn their lives to shit before I do what I'm going to do."

"Jack, why don't you just get someone—"

"BECAUSE SOMEONE ELSE DOESN'T OWE ME FUCKING MONEY, DAN! You found her, how?"

Dan said nothing.

"I said, *how?*"

"I asked around, she had a spot she would hike at.

"Hike?"

"It was luck."

Jackie chuckled through the snot rippling in his nose. "*Luck?* You found her, now find who did this. Or do you need more convincing?"

Dan stood with his one fist clenched, his other trying to curl unsuccessfully. Jackie's face was wet with the tears still falling silently down his cheeks. Dan clenched his jaw, grinding his teeth. He took a deep breath.

"Jackie, I know you're upset. And I'm sorry. Genuinely, I am. I'm sorry for your loss." He paused, trying to keep his composure. "But this has gone far enough. Be reasonable, I've done everything you've asked of me. All of it. And now I'm done."

The door behind them screeched open, metal dragging into the grooves scratched into a half circle on the ground. Annie burst through the door, trying to catch her balance as Eyebrows shoved her into the room following close behind, gun drawn, roughly grabbing at her arm above the elbow.

"You still don't understand. You're not in control of anything, and you never were. We are done when I say we're done. Not you. Find the person who did this to my little girl. Then we're done. Only then. Then you and your lady here can never see me again."

Dan was seething. "Jackie, if you touch—"

"Oh, shut the fuck up, Dan, with your tough guy bullshit. You're nothing."

He nodded to Eyebrows, who grabbed Annie's shoulder and turned her to face him and lashed his palm across her face. She stumbled, stepping back unsteadily, but didn't fall. A red hand print on her cheek, water streaming from her eyes. Dan lost his hearing—all sound focused into a high-pitched whine, a pinpoint of sound as the rage blinded him. He lunged at Jackie. After only a few steps the short goon spear tackled him like a linebacker, knocking him over the rubber bin, as the two men fell to the floor. Lydia toppled out onto the cement as the container tumbled over itself.

The goon knocked Dan's head against the ground, picking him up by his ears, knuckles smashing against the side of Dan's face. Then, scrambling behind him, he wrapped his arm around Dan's neck, the other cupping his forehead and forcing him to look at Eyebrows, who had his hand on Annie's chest, pinning her to the wall. Dan tried to process the scene, eyes still blurry from impact and rage, he heard Annie's muffled panic—moans coming out in gags as Eyebrows had his gun in her mouth, pressing it to the back of her throat. Fear broke out in a flop sweat that drenched Dan's body in an instant.

"Stop! Stop! Stop! Don't!"

Eyebrows pulled the hammer back on his gun. Annie gagged and cried. Her eyes locked onto Dan's. He'd never seen such terror in his life.

"Stop! I'll find who did this! I'll find them. I'll find

them. I'll find them. *Please.*" He began to cry. Messy sobs. Tears. Snot. Spit. All pouring from his face. His breathing was red-lined, moments from hyperventilation. *"Jackie, please."*

Jackie cleared his throat, and Eyebrows took the gun out of Annie's mouth, the color washing over her face. The barrel of the weapon backhanded her across the face, opening the bridge of her nose as Annie's knees buckled. Eyebrows caught her before she fell and shoved her violently down next to Dan. Jackie whimpered when he saw Lydia's remains lying sprawled out on the ground. Eyebrows tucked his nose into his shirt and looked away. The short man kicked at Dan, nudging him toward the remains, gagging into his hand. Dan crawled over to the container and turned it right-side up, the smell not bothering him now. His mind full of fog. He placed the remains in the container and sealed them up, wiping his hands on his pants. Jackie made no attempt to hide his crying.

"Why do you make me go through all of this, Dan?" Jackie nodded his head to Annie and snapped his fingers. His goons jumped to attention, and grabbed Annie by the arms, bringing her over to Jackie. "Find whoever did this. Find them and bring them back here, *alive*. The girl stays with us." When he stopped talking, his two men began to lead Annie roughly to the door. Eyebrows groped at Annie's backside.

"Jackie, *Jack!* Stop! Jack, stop them. I wouldn't have found Lydia without her." The words rushed out as fast as he could talk. "I need her. Jackie, if you want me to find whoever did this to your girl, I need her. You need her to help me figure this out."

"Fellas," Jackie said. The men stopped, letting go of Annie's arms. Eyebrows adjusted himself. Jackie curled his finger silently to Annie and pointed his head over to Dan, who was still on the floor. Annie knelt next to him, and Dan squeezed her hand. Jackie crouched in front of them, running his thumb and forefinger across his nose, cleaning the sadness that was draining from it. "When can you get me this person," Jackie spoke quietly, his voice crackling with phlegm from the tears crawling down his throat in a post-nasal drip. "If I let this woman go with you, how long until you can find whoever did this to my girl?"

"A lifetime Jackie, it's going to take me a fucking lifetime." Dan's voice was heavy with exhaustion, "Why don't you just go to the cops?"

"Because I don't want this man arrested. I don't want this man in jail."

"Weren't you the one who said you could kill—"

Jackie filled the room with an annoyed grunt and put his gun to Annie's temple. She let out a shriek, calling for Dan. A frantic cry of his name, then she covered her mouth, breathing into her hand. Sharp and fast inhales. Panic. Tears pouring from her face.

"If it's still going to take you a lifetime, it doesn't seem like having her will help."

Dan lunged at the gun. He grabbed Jackie's arm, and the gun fired. Then nothing. No sound. Only a high-pitched tone, narrowing to a point. The buzz rattling his mind. Annie screamed, and the goons pointed their guns at Dan, who was wrestling with Jackie, fighting for control of the pistol. The bullet shattered into a divot in the cement next to Annie, fingers in her ears, curled in a ball. Jackie rammed his knee into Dan's crotch, doubling him over, coughing. The two goons and Jackie all leveled their weapons at Dan. Their hammers locked into place.

Annie stood up and shouted, "A week! We'll find this person in a week. Give us a week. A week."

"You have five days. Pick him up." Dan hung heavily on Annie. "I still have your phone, now get," he said as Dan and Annie limped toward the door. "Dan, you're right, without her, you'd be dead."

12

THEY DIDN'T TALK WHEN THEY LEFT Jackie. Dan had to lean on Annie as he limped to the car, full of air fresheners and a stench so thick it threatened to suffocate them. Dan thought of saying something, anything, but instead he cried. And Annie cried. The whole drive was quiet except for their panicky, staggered whimpers as they tried to breathe in the space between their sobs. Annie had both of her hands covering her face as if folded in prayer. Dan wanted to reach over, rub her back, offer up some sort of comfort. Instead, he kept both hands on the wheel and drove to the motel. Comfort was pointless to either of them now.

The first thing Annie did when she got through the broken door was run to the bathroom and throw up. Retching over the toilet—her sobs stopping only long enough for her coughs to turn into liquid and pour themselves into the bowl. It happened three times, then she flushed and sat curled around the toilet, lowering the lid and resting on it like a pillow. Dan walked in and crouched next to her. He brushed her hair behind her ear and rubbed her back before running the shower. He sat on the edge of the tub, resting his elbows on his knees, hanging his head low. When the shower warmed up, he walked over to Annie and gently stroked her cheek.

"Come on, let's get clean."

Dan and Annie stood quietly in the shower, washing the wounds of each other's faces and scrubbing the scent of death and gasoline from their hands. Annie stood in the hot streams of the shower, her hands on the wall, letting the water roll down her neck, and shoulders, and back. She cupped some in her hands and gently splashed it on her face. She turned to Dan, goosebumped as the steam rose around them. He softly ran his thumb over the cut on her nose, gently placing his other on the bridge of it, and tenderly wiggled his hands. Feeling satisfied when her nose didn't budge, he let his hand fall to her cheek, moving his thumb back and forth over it, ever so slightly pinching it with each pass. His hand caressed her neck and the back of her wet, slick hair, and he leaned forward until their foreheads were touching.

He closed his eyes and listened to the hiss of the water falling on the porcelain as it sprayed over them. He cradled her hips, keeping his head against hers. Embracing. Breathing. That's when Annie's weeping broke the silence as she sobbed deep into Dan's neck. They moved closer together and he wrapped his arms around her, tears running down his chest into the water gathered by the slow drain, pink with blood. He hugged her close, and the closer he held her, the more she cried. The more she cried, the tighter he squeezed. Her cries turned to worse sobs, then back to sniffles, and then to nothing. She stood up straight and, with a crooked smile, put her forehead back against his.

"I'm done," she said with a clearing of her throat.

"Me too."

They sat on the bed in their towels, and Annie had worked her hands back and forth roughly through the one bunched around her hair. Dan sat with his head down, looking at his thigh sticking through the slit of his towel at the smooth skin breaking through the wispy curls. Annie's hair stuck off her head in stringy, damp strands. She was having a hard time looking at Dan, her face tired and vacant.

"That was so scary," she said.

"You never should have been in that situation." He let out a sigh that dripped with exhaustion. "I'm sorry."

"I was always involved. But now I'm..." she bulged her eyes, "...*involved*." She looked at him, stained in regret. "Dan, we almost died tonight. I've nev—I've never had a gun—" Her voice broke, so she cleared her throat. "There's no reasoning with him is there?"

"No."

"He'll never let us go."

"No." Dan let out a frustrated grunt that dripped with their shared pain. Then, in defeat, he asked, "How are we going to find this person?"

"Do we have to? If he's never going to let us go."

Dan exhaled slowly through his nose, then pleaded quietly, "Don't tempt me." He put his hand on her knee, and Annie took it in hers. "He knows who you are now, and he knows where you work. Everyone there is in danger, and my family. I'm sure he can figure out your family, too. Fuck, why did I let you cancel that Uber?"

"Trevor."

"What?"

"I can't go back to him now, not like this. How can I explain this to him, all my cuts and bruises?"

Dan lay back on the bed and put his hands over his face. Annie stared up at the ceiling next to him. He lifted his hand to looked at her. "Do you hate me?"

"Hate?" She looked at him, then turned back to the ceiling before taking a deep breath. The silence between his question and her answer hung longer than he was comfortable with, and his face prickled with needles, knowing the answer leaned in a direction he feared. She gently squeezed his hand. "No, I don't hate you. It's more complicated." It was hard, but Dan looked her in her eyes as she continued. "Up until a few days ago, you were a guy that came into the diner, ordered the usual, we'd flirt, and that would be it. And I always liked it when you came in, a lot. Some days I couldn't get to work fast enough. I felt this, *I don't know,* a kind of electricity between us. Excitement I craved. This spark. A fire in me I thought was dead. Then you come in and you're hurt, so I help. I don't know why I volunteered to help you find Lydia, I really don't. You explained how severe it was, but I don't know why I didn't listen. It seemed like an adventure, some fun mystery. A game, almost. I don't hate you. But I wish I hadn't offered to help."

Dan was crying. Annie looked back at the ceiling and continued. "I know I said I don't regret what's happened with us, the, well, the physical stuff." She cleared her throat, and the pause stretched for an eternity. "But now, maybe, I guess after everything, I wish I hadn't gotten involved at all. I'm sorry. I wish we had what we have—the good parts. But not this. I care about you. And I really do wish, *I do,* I wish that we just did the whole damn thing unattached to any of this. I wish I wasn't married, that's what I wish. I wasn't married, and you came in, and you weren't hurt or bandaged, just you. And you'd flirt with me, and I flirt back, and you asked me out somewhere after work, and everything happened as it happened. The dancing, the drinking, the sex, the showers—that's what I want. I wish I had never got involved with Lydia. With Jackie. *I can still taste that gun, Dan.* On my tongue, I can taste it. I can't get it out of my mouth. The back of my throat hurts when I swallow. My hearing is going in and out. I'm so scared, and I don't know what to do. I can't go home, I don't know what to tell anyone. What to tell Trevor. I don't know. I'm stuck."

Dan said nothing. He put a hand over his eyes, now glassy with remorse. His breath staggered on his inhale, and he exhaled quietly, his lips trembling, puckered in an O-shape.

Annie squeezed his hand and with her other removed his hand from his eyes, seeing the water pooled in the corner of them, falling silently down his temples and past his ear. "But, Dan, if I'm stuck, I am glad I'm stuck with you. I'm glad it's me and you that have to figure this out. I don't hate you, hun." She gently turned his chin to face her. "I just regret meeting you, is all." The joke momentarily broke the tension and made them laugh harder than it should have with the relief of it.

"I don't know what to do," he said, his voice cracking before it broke. "I'm so sorry for all of this. I'm so dumb. I'm so, so," his voice shattered, "goddamn useless." The cries came out in loud, uncontrollable sobs. He rolled on his side towards her and brought his knees to his chest, curling into a ball. She wrapped her arms around him as he lay his head, face in hands, on her chest. Her skin, warm and soft. She made *shh*-ing sounds and stroked his hair with her fingertips. Whispering *it's okay, shh* over and over as she held him. The tears dripped across her chest and along her collar bone.

I know Dan, I know.

In his dream, Annie died. Jackie had his gun in her mouth and was dragging her across the floor with it. Blood serpentining in a trail behind them as Jackie lumbered forward. Annie slid across the ground on her back like a snake, vomiting up the barrel into Jackie's palm. In the fleeting moments where, even in his sleep, Dan knew it was only a dream, hoping maybe he had dozed off while they were fooling around, maybe it was him in Annie's mouth, not Jackie's pistol—that none of these horrors were real and they were happy in bed together. But there was no mixture of reality slipping into this. Only nightmare. Dan chased after them but never gained any ground. No matter how fast he ran, Jackie only walked. Further and further away. Calm. Steady. Slow. All he could do was follow the line of blood. Jackie overlooked the hillside where Lydia's body had been, now empty and dark. Dan watched as Jackie lifted his arm, pulling Annie to his face. He grabbed her by the throat, and threw her tumbling down the hill. She landed limp and lifeless where Lydia once lay. Insects and birds swarmed her, coyotes ripping her apart. Her head rolled to the side, and she stared unbroken at Dan as the beaks pecked through her cheeks, and ears, and face.

Dan opened his eyes.

Annie's head was on his chest, her body rising slowly, rhythmic with sleep. He didn't want to wake her, so he looked at the ceiling. The soundless blue light from the TV moved around the tiles, and the fan blades cut long shadows across the tiles to the wall. The image of Jackie throwing Annie into Lydia's shallow grave looped in his head like a broken movie reel, continually flickering through his mind. Seeing her fall slack with a thud, rolling down the hill, with a hole blown through the back of her head, caked red with bloody dirt. Her body, curled and wilted, eyes pale and foggy. She stared at him. Then the movie played over again. And again. And again. Dan watched as the shadows on the tile shifted and shrank—an orange and yellow glow crawling up the walls spreading across the ceiling as the sun seeped in through the curtains. Annie jumped and lifted her head, wiping the back of her hand across her mouth.

"How'd you sleep?" Her voice croaked, still in a dreamy haze.

"Like shit, you?"

"Not very good." She sat up and stretched, her back arching and fists clenched, wrists turned in. A shiver worked up her body and puckered her face. "I kept getting anxiety about having a concussion, so I was scared to sleep. But I must have tired myself out worrying because here we are."

"And you woke up, so—"

"No concussion."

"No concussion."

"I'm too tired for real life to start up," Annie said.

"And not drunk enough."

"Dangerously sober."

"Are you hungry?"

"Very." She paused. "My face, does it look bad?"

"Not great."

"Can we order something? I don't want to deal with the looks."

"What time is it? I'll head to the gas station and get us some beer."

Dan clumsily squeezed himself through the door of the motel holding a plastic bag of takeout and a six-pack of beer. Annie was sitting in a chair with her knees tucked into the shirt she was wearing as a nightgown, her eyes puffy and wet. She told him she called Trevor to say she wouldn't be coming home. She said she couldn't explain why, but that she had gotten herself into trouble and needed to stay away. She told Dan that he asked if there was another man, and that she said yes. Trevor asked if she was pregnant, and she said it wasn't that kind of trouble. She wished he would have cursed her out, called her a whore. She hoped that he was seeing someone too. She wanted Trevor to hurt her and snap, help her feel better about it, like she wasn't being a horrible person, that he deserved this.

But all Trevor said was "I see," and told her that he hoped she got herself sorted out and was safe. And that he hoped she would come home, regardless of any trouble she was in. But he knew she wouldn't. So, he wished her luck, and that was that. No anger, no guilt, no lashing out, and no *I love you*. Annie was glad about that, but also hurt. She was crying, but Trevor didn't seem to be, and then he hung up.

Dan didn't know what to say. He put everything down on the table, knelt in front of the chair, and placed his hands on the outside of her thighs as she talked—watching her blink back her tears, looking to the ceiling to keep them from falling down her cheeks. He wished he could hide the emotions on his face, knowing it wouldn't help her to see it. He pinched her chin between his thumb and forefinger, wiping away a hanging tear, then kissed her head and told her to eat, that she'd feel better.

Annie rolled her pancake like a thick cigar and dipped it into a small plastic cup of syrup, moaning loudly with delight as she chewed.

"Wow. These are incredible," she said. "So good, like, the best pancake I've ever had. I feel like I'm high or something."

"Almost dying must do that. The first breakfast you got me when I showed up all beaten and bleeding, it was heaven."

"First meal of the rest of our lives."

Dan sipped his beer, anxiously spinning the can on the ring of condensation it dripped on the table. He stabbed at the yolk of his egg, then pressed it so the yolk bled from the punctures.

"About this whole thing, I was thinking last night," he said, dipping a piece of rye toast into the yolk and chipmunking it in his cheek after chewing. "Lydia loved that spot, right? And it wasn't that easy to get to. It doesn't seem likely that many people would find their way up there to go hiking. Maybe a few here and there, but we didn't see anyone, right? It's just, I was thinking." He finished chewing and washed it down with some more beer. Annie looked up from her pancake, waiting for him to swallow. "The odds of someone randomly stumbling upon her and also that person being a random murderer have to be pretty slim, right?"

"I would think so," Annie said, covering her mouth with her hand as she spoke.

"I'm sure it happens, but it just seems impossibly slim. I guess with our luck, that means that's exactly what happened. Some random person, and we'll never be able to find them. But for right now, for our sanity, it feels too slim."

"You think the person knew her?"

"That's what I'm thinking. Whoever did this knew her enough—"

"Enough that they knew where to find her," Annie said.

"Or they went together."

"So, close enough that she shared that place."

"Pretty thin, right?"

"Thin, but it's something."

"But where does that leave us?"

Annie sat back and rubbed her waist.

"So full," she said, and took a swig of beer. "We have three leads." She crooked her thumb, "Jimmy the Saint," she popped up her pointer finger, and hesitated.

"Johnny Boy, the tattoo guy."

"Thank you," she raised her middle finger. "And the kid from New York with the dreads and stupid nickname."

"Predator?"

"No, dumber."

"Oh, Medusa, right?"

"That sounds right."

"He's kind of a non-starter, because I don't think we can get to New York."

"Wandering around some strange city looking for a guy who may or may not have dreadlocks."

"Right," she said with a chuckle. "Oh, and a scar, don't forget that." They shared a laugh. "So that leaves us, Johnny Boy, then."

"What about Jimmy?" said Dan, eyebrows crooked in confusion.

"He's the one who told us about that place. Why would he do that?"

"A misdirection?"

"Except we had no direction," she said. "Why would he lead us there if he could just not have said anything?"

"Who was that other guy they named? Rick?"

"Quick Rich," she said with a grin. "They didn't seem to think he was anyone. That one guy hated him, maybe he's something, we can put him on the list, but either way, I think the first stop would be to see Johnny Boy."

Dan rubbed his hands over his face with annoyance. "What the fuck are these names? The kids today have all these stupid fucking nicknames." They both laughed. "Quick Dick, Saint Tommy, Joey Chestnuts or whatever."

"I think the last one is a professional hot dog eater."

Dan felt a grin rise across his face, looking at Annie with the dark circles under her eyes and the cut across her nose, with the sun lighting up half her face so angelically from the gap between the curtains, the thin t-shirt draping over the curves of her chest. "Johnny Boy, it is."

13

THE SHOP WAS LOUD AS HELL WITH THE buzzing and music, and the artists talking over all of it. The music was different from the first time they were there, classic rock instead of metal, which was already more pleasing. The woman at the front desk was friendly when the door chimed, but her face changed when she saw the two of them bruised and cut up. Focusing on Annie's face, then glancing at Dan's.

"Do you have an appointment?"

"We need to speak to Johnny Boy. We were in the other day," said Dan.

The woman behind the desk cleared her throat. "Let me go get him." She walked over to where he was hunched over someone's leg, drilling into their shin with his machine. The man in the chair was sweating, eyes bulging like they were falling out of his face.

"You guys look like shit," he shouted, looking up from his work.

"It's been a hell of a night. We were wondering if we could ask you some more questions," Dan shouted back.

"Can it wait?" He turned back to the leg and called over his shoulder. "Did you find her?" The silence that hung around the question grew until it became deafening, overpowering the other sounds of the shop. Johnny Boy looked back at Dan and shared the same knowing look. "I'll be with you once I'm done with this. I just started. It'll be a while if you guys wanna come back."

"We'll wait here."

Dan and Annie sat on the cracked leather couches and flipped through the different books of the artists in the shop. Dan pointed to one of the photos. "I know that girl," he said. "She works at the gas station by me and won't sell me beer if it's too early." Annie continued to mindlessly flip through the books as Dan got up and strolled along the wall, looking at the flash work.

"Dan, come here! Look." She wasn't excited, but she was close to it. She had Johnny Boy's portfolio splayed open by the spine, pointing to a photo of Johnny coloring the solid blank ink of Lydia's arm. She was grimacing in pain, but also laughing, so was Johnny, mid-conversation, hunched over her triceps. "She looks happy here." Dan noted the yellow timestamp in the corner, three years ago. "It's weird seeing her like this."

A song from the 50s came over the speakers with some guitar and light drums—tight harmonies with two male voices, but the name escaped Dan. Annie closed the book and returned it to the shelf with the other portfolios. She told Dan about when she was little, how she had a babysitter named Suzie, and they'd always sing this song to her, and how she would laugh.

"Being older now, though," Annie said, "I have to give her credit. I can't imagine how annoying it must have been for kids who aren't even yours to keep singing this to you over and over. Patience of a saint."

"It's weird," Dan said. "You wouldn't picture music that sounds like this to be, I dunno, like these guys had big big drug problems, and you wouldn't think it listening to them. It's so clean-sounding. Not the quality, but like, *Leave-It-to-Beaver*-type of clean. You know?"

She laughed. "Leave It to Beaver clean, I swear, Dan, the way your mind works." The two stepped outside, setting off the door chime, the sounds of the shop fading as the door closed behind them. Replaced now with the passing cars and how they sounded like crashing ocean waves as they drove past. The two sat on the sidewalk and smoked cigarettes, watching the vehicles and talking about the type of people in them. How some were probably sweet, or maybe they were boring just working for IRS or something, never so much as a speeding ticket to their name, but some of the drivers passing by were probably into weird fetishes, or maybe have killed someone, like how they drove down the street with Lydia in their trunk, a whole dark world tucked into their car. They joked about how some were off to a hotel where they all dressed up like stuffed animals and masturbated in a circle, but here they were, driving by all nameless and faceless. A glimpse of a person, no features, only dark glasses or a tie seen through the windows as they zoom past. Completely unknown and anonymous. Anyone could be anyone.

Annie crouched in a half-stand, looking through the window at Johnny Boy still working away, the man in the chair squirming. She sat back down and looked at the light grey cement and the cigarettes in the gutter. She picked up a butt and drew a number sign on the cement, dark grey ash, adding an X in the center. Dan smiled and gathered his ashes to draw a circle. Annie beat him a few moves later, running her fingers over three Xs in a row, blending them together in a dark smudge.

"Know what I was thinking this morning, when I picked up the beer," Dan said, wiping his finger on his jeans. Annie doing the same to the inside of her pant leg. "When I was leaving, the guy behind the counter said, what was it, *by-a cone dee-o*, something like that. That means goodbye, right?"

Annie's thumbs worked over the screen of her phone, a quick vibrating buzz with each letter pressed, getting mixed into the sound of the wind and passing cars. *Tap, tap, tap.* "Vaya con Dios," she said. "Go with God."

"That's it," Dan said, his eyebrows lifting with brief excitement. "Vaya con Dios. *Go with God.* It felt peaceful." He lit a cigarette, his voice softer and higher, as he tried to let the words out but keep the smoke in. "We don't really have anything like that in English, do we? We always say something like *See you later*, or some boring shit." He passed the cigarette to Annie.

"Catch you on the flip side," she said, the cigarette pinched delicately in her fingers, the round edge of the butt resting on her lower lip, one eye in a squint against the smoke. "You could just say *Go with God* in English."

"I guess, but it's not the same. That just sounds like you're translating something cooler. It's not as sincere," he said. "Peace out, maybe. Because of the peace. That feels like a stretch, though."

"See you later, alligator."

"Hasta la vista, baby."

"That's Spanish again," Annie said, smoke clumsily escaping her mouth as she laughed, coughing the rest of it into her fist. Dan joined in.

Annie passed him the rest of the cigarette. "In a while, crocodile."

Dan finished the smoke and flicked the filter into the parking lot as they watched the cars passing by with their secret lives. One drove by blasting a ska song they both recognized from a game they played when they were younger. Annie sat back and started to sing what she remembered of it. The last few days left Dan in a blur of reality—a detachment where he was so focused on staying alive and keeping Annie safe that he didn't have time to think. He was underwater, getting knocked down by waves of confusion and panic, then back to reality for a moment, gasping for air and looking for help before the next wave would crash over him, sending him flailing once more, wondering how long before he would be able to breathe again. Over and over. And over. But, in this moment, with the ash slicing through her Tic-Tac-Toe victory and the soft, airy tone of her singing their half-remembered song, it made him realize just how much he didn't want to die.

Dan stood up and wiped the dirt and grit from his backside, and looked in the window. Johnny Boy was rubbing his fingers over the tattoo, before wrapping it in cellophane and masking tape.

"I think he's done."

* * *

"That looked painful," Annie said. "It's all bone."

Johnny Boy chuckled, "Good. He was annoying. And cheap. Fuck him." They all sat on the couches in the lobby, the music still playing oldies. Johnny Boy had his legs crossed with his ankle resting on his other knee, holding his shin. "So, you found Lydia," he said, surprisingly loud. "And I'm assuming—"

Annie shook her head, mouth in a tight grimace, grief overtaking her face.

"It's messy," Dan said.

"And all of this," Johnny Boy pointed to the cuts and bruises on their faces.

"It's part of the mess," he said.

Johnny Boy nodded, satisfied. A realization struck him. "Wait, do you think I had something to do with it?"

"No," she said, her voice loud with overcompensation.

Dan looked over his shoulder and hushed his voice, leaning over to Johnny Boy. "We don't think you had anything to do with it. But also," he looked around again, "I don't actually care. I'm not a cop, I didn't know her."

Annie frowned. "Do you know anyone who might have seen her? Do you remember the last time you saw her?"

"It's been forever. And we weren't even that close."

"I thought you two dated," Annie said.

"We hooked up. It wasn't anything more than that. The only thing that kept it from being some anonymous one-night stand was that it happened more than once, but it was the same thing."

The door chimed, and Slate came in carrying a cardboard box of drinks and sandwiches wrapped in white wax paper. He gave the girl behind the desk her order and walked over to the couches. "You guys again," he said, not looking at them until after he gave Johnny Boy his food. "Jesus, the fuck happened?" He pointed to Annie. "You didn't do that, did you?"

"No, it happened to both of us. We were jumped," Dan said.

"Lydia is dead," Johnny Boy burst out, biting into his sandwich, mayo on his chin, and lettuce falling into his lap.

"Sorry to hear it," Slate said. "She seemed like an okay girl. I question her taste sometimes, but she seemed nice enough."

"Thanks," Dan said, but didn't know why.

"Do you guys know a Dusa?" Annie said. "Or maybe Medusa?"

Slate and Johnny Boy looked at each other, stumped.

"They are the only other person we have a name for that might have known her. Jimmy mentioned him, but that's all we know," Annie said.

"I never heard of him. Do you know what he looks like?" Slate peeled back the wrapper of his sandwich.

Dan and Annie looked at each other, trying to recall a shared memory. "Dreadlocks," Dan said. "From New York, we think." Slate and Johnny Boy looked at each other again, their eyebrows furrowed in confusion.

"And a scar," Annie said.

Slate swallowed a bite too big for him and winced. "That's Quick Rich. Fuck that guy."

"Slate gave him that scar," said Johnny Boy.

"I should have done more." He looked at Annie and

Dan's perplexed faces. "He tried to rob the shop with a box cutter. I should have tattooed SCUMBAG across his fucking forehead."

"Wait, Dusa and Quick Rich are the same person?" Dan said, his wide-eyed stare matching Annie's.

"I don't know who calls him Dusa, maybe New York folks," Johnny Boy said. "We always called him Quick Rich because he was always planning some sort of get-rich-quick scheme, you know?"

Dan shifted his body. "I know the type."

"Do you happen to know where we might be able to find this Rich?" Annie said.

"Slate, you saw him the other day, right? At the drug store." Slate looked at Johnny Boy. "When you were picking up gloves until our shipment came."

"Is Rich his real name?" Annie said.

"Yes, and yes," Slate said. "He was standing outside asking people if they had change for a hundred-dollar bill. He got a haircut, though, no more dreads."

"He's not in New York, he's here?" Excitement rose in Annie's voice.

"Why didn't he get change from the store?" Dan said.

"I don't know, man, it's Quick Rich, what do you want? He's always got something cooking," Slate said, and took another bite of his sandwich.

"Do you know where he lives? Or where he's staying?" Annie said.

"I only spoke to him long enough to tell him to get away from me," Slate said.

"Don't look at me," Johnny Boy said, wiping his mouth on the back of his hand. "I haven't seen him since the robbery."

"Attempted," Slate said. "He didn't walk away with shit, except that scar."

Annie gently grabbed Dan's hand, interlacing her fingers with his. "Could you tell us where this drug store is?"

14

THEY HUNG AROUND THE DRUG STORE for a little over an hour. They didn't know what Quick Rich looked like, but figured they'd recognize him when they saw them. "I feel like you can just tell when someone used to have dreadlocks, you can see it in their haircut," Annie had said when Dan began to get frustrated at being one step closer, but no closer at all. He kept it inside because he knew how tired it made Annie, but he couldn't let himself get too comfortable in daydreaming about success. After this then Jackie will find some other reason, and then another reason, then another. Threatening Annie, and Dan's mom, his sister. Hell, he'd probably go after Annie's husband, too, just because. Dan didn't know how he felt about that, but he knew he'd hate to see her so torn up. The anxiety grew like water behind a dam, Dan's hands fidgeting and leg bouncing. Annie gave him a knowing smile and put her hand on his thigh, which slowed and eventually stopped shaking altogether.

Annie couldn't believe that the smell was still lingering. The body was only in the car for a few hours, not even, and was in a bag, in another bag, in a sealed rubber container. She pulled one of the many trees hanging from the mirror and pressed it to her nose, smelling it, crinkling in the cute way it does, almost cartoonish. The cut across the bridge was a dark scab now, pink around the edges with freshness. She looked in the glove box, shuffling through the contents, finding nothing she was searching for, and told Dan that she would pop into the store quickly to try and get more air fresheners. She checked the back seat, hoping maybe there was a cap or sunglasses, anything to hide her face to avoid any stares. Dan offered to go in for her, but Annie said she wanted to stretch her legs and that she'd ignore any weird glances. She told Dan to keep an eye out for someone with a scar that looked like he used to have dreadlocks, and she'd do the same when she's in the store. They both laughed, then she squeezed his hand and left.

Dan waited until she disappeared into the store and turned down the only aisle he could see through the glass of the storefront before he released all the anxiety and frustration he had bottled up. Slamming his body back and forth, cursing up a barrage of nonsense, spit flying from his mouth. He grabbed the wheel and started cranking it side to side before gripping it and screaming into the center of it. He was out of breath and crying. He quickly wiped his eyes and mouth with his sleeve, pinching at the drops falling from his nose.

Deep breaths. Deep, slow breaths.

The opening of the passenger-side door startled him, making him jump.

"Sorry," Annie said. She was holding a bottle of air freshener and sprayed the mist into the back seat and floor. "This was all they had. No car fresheners at all. I saw the spot for them, but they were completely sold out."

It didn't help, and the car smelled like dead bodies wrapped in fresh linen.

They gave up on the drug store and decided to return early in the morning and spend the day in the area looking for him. The car ride to the motel was quiet. An exhausted quiet. A quiet that was as close as talking. Annie rested her head on the window as Dan drove. They pulled into the spot in front of Dan's room, and the headlights shone on the broken, crooked door. He turned the car off and got out. The overhead light went dark, but Annie didn't move. Dan opened his door again, the light popping on. Annie was wiping her cheeks. He slid back into his seat and moved close to her. The car was dark again.

He put his arm around her, but she didn't turn to him right away. "Dan, I'm scared."

"Me too," he said. "We'll figure it out, we'll find him."

"No." She turned to him and ran the heel of her palm under her eye. Her face was discolored, purple and green. "I'm scared they'll come back. They have me so terrified. I don't want to die, Dan."

"I don't know what we can do. We'll barricade it from the inside, more than just the dresser. We'll move everything."

"All day, Dan, all day, I wasn't scared. I thought about it, but I wasn't afraid. It was just a memory, and I could deal with that, you know? But now. Now I'm—I can't go in there, I can't. Like, physically. I don't think I can get out of the car. I don't know what to do."

He squeezed her shoulder and held her close to his chest. She rested her head on his neck.

"Can we stay somewhere else?" Annie said, soft in a whisper. "I can get us a hotel room. They won't know where to look or how to find us. We can get a room on a high floor with deadbolts, and chains, and hotel security."

Dan wouldn't be happy letting her foot the bill, but knew he couldn't swing it. He could barely afford the beer and breakfast this morning. But he hated seeing her like this—crying and scared. Bruised, face swollen, and all because he got her into this whole fucking goddamn mess. He'd find a way to make it up to her, but right now she needed rest, and for that she needed safety.

The hotel was nicer than any place Dan had ever stayed before. A fountain filled with koi, and a bar with a glass front and a piano player in the lobby. The bar was full of men in suits standing around drinking beers and draping their arms around girls who were giving each other side eyes and covering their drinks with their hands—only tolerating the men to avoid the scarier bunch of rowdy college kids doing shots at the bar, bringing down the class of the place. All of the normal rooms were taken, so Annie got them a fancier suite on a high floor with a balcony and a sitting area. The bed was a full two sizes bigger than the one in Dan's room, and this door didn't only close, but had a deadbolt, a doorknob lock, and a swing bar which kept it from opening more than a few inches. As soon as they entered the room, Annie engaged all of the locking mechanisms. It felt like they could breathe again. The hotel was on the outskirts of the city, close enough that they could still see the lights and billboards and headlights from the traffic in the distance, but the glow from all of it faded before it reached the balcony—unable to survive the darkness of the desert and the black sky with its bright pinholes of white light like salt spilled over a black tablecloth. The sound of the wind and the cars poured through the open sliding glass door into their room.

Dan sat on the bed and kicked off his shoes, flipping on the TV with the remote sitting on the Bible in the drawer of the nightstand. The TV was set to a classic movie station when it turned on, and Steve McQueen was jumping a motorcycle over hills and fences of barbed wire while Nazi's shot at him. The water ran in the bathtub, pouring loudly from the faucet, splashing against the ivory-white tub. Annie stood in the threshold of the bathroom and unhooked her bra.

"Wanna join?"

Dan's stumbled over his shoes. Unbuttoning his pants before she even finished her question.

In the shower they washed the dust and sweat of the day from each other and Dan used his thumb to clean the cuts on her face. They kissed and moved their slick soap-covered hands over each other, leaving trails of suds rolling off them in the spray of the water. Dan kissed her breast briefly, and Annie started to use her hand on him, but they lost interest before anything developed. Too tired and sore to make anything last. Annie told him she would help him if he was too worked up, or he could just do it, she didn't mind watching. Dan told her it was more effort than he had in him at the moment. They tried to muster the energy one last time with the same result, and ended up giggling into each other's mouths, making jokes through their teeth between each kiss. Dan got out of the shower, but Annie stayed in, saying she liked the hot water beating on her back. Dan dried off, wrapped his towel around his waist, and sat on the toilet. He worked the fingers and muscles in his bad hand to try and see how much movement he had. The laces and creases of the brace were still indented into his swollen skin.

"That doesn't seem to be getting any better." Annie peeked out of the sliding glass door, leaving it mostly open.

"I aggravated it today," Dan said with embarrassment. "When you were in the store. I freaked out a bit."

Annie looked concerned.

"It's fine," he said, and brushed her look away with his hand. "The same shit."

"About us?"

"Maybe, sort of? But mostly Jackie. And about how this is never going to stop."

"I'm scared too," Annie said. "I'm good at blocking it out during the day, but it always seems to catch up."

"Yes, it does."

Annie tilted her head back and let the water run over her hair, running her hands over it, combing it with her fingers. "What was your first job?" she said.

Dan didn't answer. Annie watched his face contort in confusion as he tried to process the abrupt change of topic.

"Your first job," she said. "As a kid, or teenager, or whatever. Where'd you work?"

"Blockbuster Video, why?" Dan said.

"Just wondering." She straightened her head and stayed in the hot stream of the shower, hunched toward the water jets. "How long did you work there?"

"A few months," Dan said. "I got fired."

"Oh, the plot thickens."

Dan laughed. "Once I figured out how to get rid of people's late fees, I was doing it for everyone. Late fees were such a racket," he said. "I couldn't stand people paying for another three-day rental just because they were a few hours late. Give these people a break, you know? You can only do that so many times before your boss has had enough. What was your first job?"

"A thrift store. When I was in high school. Nothing as glamorous as being the Robin Hood of Blockbuster."

Dan's chuckle escaped his mouth unexpectedly, and he couldn't stop giggling. "Blockbuster's Robin Hood—I like that," he said. "Are you going to stay in there all day?"

"I haven't decided. I might!" she said and turned to face the water.

"Isn't it too hot? This place looks like a sauna, look how red your skin is."

"No such thing as a shower that's too hot," she said.

"Thrift stores hire people?"

"Of course they do, what'd you think?"

"That it was a volunteer gig," Dan said.

"Some are maybe, not that one though. I did try volunteering once, at an animal shelter. I only lasted a few days because I got too attached to the animals, which you're not supposed to do. I couldn't take it when they had to be, well, you know. I tried to save them, but there's only so much you can do."

"I don't know how people can—"

"Oh wait!" Annie said. "I have something sort of interesting. It's no Robin Hood or anything, but it's pretty unique, I think. I don't know if you'd even say it was a job, maybe it was. But I was on one of those public access shows as a kid. Not on PBS or anything, more local."

"Really?" he said. "Annie, the child star!"

"Hardly," she laughed. "It was one of those science shows, almost like Bill Nye or Mr. Wizard. Did you ever watch those?"

"I'm sure I did. I don't remember, though."

"This one was super low budget. It was me and maybe two other kids. This is like thirty years ago, so I barely remember myself. I don't even know if it paid. Maybe my parents got money? Or I got some sort of savings account or something. Don't they do that for kids? Anyway, I only remember one episode. It was about electricity and about being grounded. I only remember because he talked about how squirrels can run on wires because they are only touching one. But if they touched the other one also, they'd get electrocuted."

"Birds too, I suppose."

"Anything on a wire, probably. He did this experiment with a taxidermied—is that a word? *Taxidermied?*—A stuffed squirrel. And he had these model of telephone poles set up. But something happened, and when he touched both wires with the animal, there was a pop, and everything went dark, and then these red flood lights came on. All the cameras and TV stuff shut down. Ruined the whole episode. Friends at school told me they needed to put up one of those technical difficulties signs and everything. Maybe he wasn't that good of a scientist. The Video Wizard. Even the name was low budget." Annie let out a laugh that was mostly air, a *pfft*. "Video Wizard, *so dumb*."

The water turned off, and for a moment, the bathroom was church-quiet. Then drips from the shower head began to fall onto the faucet below and splash into the water pooling by the drain. Annie slid the door open fully, and the steam hung in the air behind her, shifting like fog, rising off her shoulders. Dan handed her a towel, and she dried herself off, wrapping it around her head before stepping out of the tub. She slid into one of the bathrobes hanging from the door and leaned on the sink, next to where Dan was sitting.

"What's with the look?" Annie said.

"I'm just confused," he said. "I was expecting these stories to go some place. It's just random, is all."

Annie roughed her towel over Dan's hair. "Nothing more to it. I'm just over talking about the other stuff anymore. If I never have to talk about us or Jackie or Trevor again, I'd be happy as a log. I guess I was a bit heavy-handed with it."

"I don't think that's the saying."

"Really? *Happy as a log,* that's not it? Have I been saying it wrong my whole life? They just sit there, happy and covered in moss. Whatever, who cares. They rob too much of my time as it is."

"No, you're right. Sometimes my mind can get very... stuck," he said and took the towel off of his head. "I wish it didn't."

"I get that way too, sometimes," she said. "It doesn't seem to be helping if we're both in it at the same time."

"We need to ground ourselves," Dan said with a smile.

Annie let out a loud laugh that amplified the quiet bathroom with an echo.

"Look at that," she said. "Completely unplanned, but still. No, I mean...that was the whole point, this whole time. Completely intentional, totally." Annie thought for a moment, "Hmm, so we're both wires, me and you, and—I don't know what—Sadness? Anxiety? Jackie? Whatever it is, is the squirrel. I guess that seems about right. Okay, I like this. And it can't touch us both at the same time. Or else," she grabbed his legs and started shaking them, *bzzzz*.

"Then we'd want to electrocute the squirrel, though." Dan fought to stay defeated. He tried to pass it off as joking the best he could, but wasn't sure why he was trying to dismantle this. He hid it behind a wry grin. "Or, wouldn't we be the squirrels? And the wires would be Jack—"

"We're the wires. We need to stay grounded. Wires are what get grounded, not the squirrels, right?"

"But, if the squirrel was grounded, then he'd—"

"Whatever, it's not perfect. I'm making it up as I go," she laughed. "What I'm saying, jerk, is we need to find a way for us to not both be fucked up over this at the same time. So whatever combination of us and squirrels and wires and Jackie and all of that—however that equals that—is where we have to get to."

"I don't think it's in our control."

"Stop being so difficult." She playfully pinched his knee and watched him squirm and pretend it didn't tickle. "Of course it isn't. But we can fake it until we make it," she said. "So, here's the plan."

"There's a plan?"

"You have tonight to just be in the shit, stare into the abyss—all of that—and I'll keep watch." She nudged his foot to get his attention. He smiled weakly back at her, defeat still painting his face. "You freak out and let your mind go to the dark places, and I'll stay outside and force optimism."

"Can you do that?"

"Sure," she said. "A few years ago, me and Trevor tried couples therapy. Everything felt like an attack to him." She shook her head, her face scrunched in embarrassment. She used her hands to try and erase the awkward mention of her husband from the air, "Anyway, obviously it didn't work, but I kept going on my own. She'd have a field day with me if she knew about *this*."

"Why'd you stop going?"

"Money. Stop trying to change the subject. One week, she gave me this exercise to do where you write down the shitty things in your life, one a day, but then you also write down one good aspect too, a silver lining, to that thing. It's supposed to train our minds. We don't have to go as extreme, I'm just saying we can do that. But we'll double team it. Take turns, so you see the shitty stuff today, and I'll find the silver lining. And then tomorrow it's my turn, and you help me with the good things."

"Do you think that'll work?"

"If you ask tomorrow then I'd say no, not at all. But tonight? Sure, it'll work. No doubt." She offered him her hands, and he took them. He kissed her. She crinkled her nose and said, "I want to order some room service, I think."

"It's expensive, I can go pick us up something," Dan said.

"No," she said, smiling and lightly stomping as if she were putting her foot down. "Let's treat ourselves."

By the time they were done in the bathroom, the movie on TV changed to another World War II movie from the 60s. No more Steve McQueen, but this one also had Charles Bronson in it, which Annie pointed out. The remote was too far away for either of them to reach, so the two sat on the bed, forced by their comfort to keep watching. They were still wet from the shower and wrapped in the white fluffy bathrobes of the hotel suite. Annie's hair, damp and hanging in loose curls, draped over Dan's chest as she leaned her head on his shoulder. She pressed her body closer to his as they watched the handful of army prisoners build a barracks. Her knee was up and sliced through the front of her robe, the terrycloth belt loosening its hold. The inside of her thigh was smooth and soft with a few thumb prints of cellulite. Dan could see most of her breasts as the robe kept slipping open.

Annie ordered French fries and beer, and Dan a steak sandwich. When they finished, they set the plates on the tray next to them, leaving only crumbs and spatterings of ketchup and steak sauce, with some bitten fry ends, and salt.

"Do you think this is anyone's favorite movie?" Annie didn't look away from the TV, where Lee Marvin was shooting someone trying to climb a rope. He hit the rope so all the slack behind the man was gone, and he had no choice but to keep climbing. The movie was sped up to make it seem like the soldier was climbing faster than he was.

"Of course," Dan said with a level of disbelief in his voice. "This movie is really famous. It's a classic."

"But it's *so slow*," Annie dragged the words out.

"A lot of movies from this time were."

"It's so boring, I just don't get how it can be someone's favorite. How could you even rewatch it?"

"Is that what makes a movie your favorite? The number of times you rewatch it?"

"That should be a qualification, I think. I'm not sure if it's the most important thing, but it's up there."

"What else?"

She scrunched her face, thinking. "Hmm, a certain level of comfort, too."

"Comfort," Dan said, more than asked.

"Comfort. You should feel relaxed and at home with it, like it's a warm bath."

Dan never thought about what makes a movie a favorite. He wasn't sure if comfort was a factor, but he didn't want to disagree with her. She seemed to be enjoying this game, and he heard a relaxed cuteness in her voice—a tone he hadn't heard in a while. One she used to have. A higher pitch with a melody of hope in it. It was a quality she lost the moment she saw Lydia in the sand. A warmth came over him, hearing it again. The same feeling that would hit him when she would take his order and linger to make small talk. That unspoken energy that was between them. A spark and rapport that went deeper than flirting. Subtext and electricity. Before he robbed her of that by getting her involved with Jackie and his two fucking goons, breaking apart a dead body in the pitch-black desert, and reeking of decay. But he heard it now and never wanted her to stop talking.

"I feel like," she said, "and don't judge me for thinking it," she lifted her head from his shoulder and sat up taller, a smile growing on her face. "I feel like so many people lie when they talk about their favorite movie. They want to impress people, so they act like theirs are deeper and more special. They'll pick some movie they saw that they probably didn't even fully get, but it made them feel unique, or fancy. So, they'll say their favorite movie is some sort of French movie from the 60s that's all just cigarettes and museums and crying babies looking at balloons that no one's ever heard of, and they'll never watch it again. Not even when it's on TV. And that doesn't make sense to me. How can that be your favorite?" She pointed at the screen and put her head back on his shoulder.

"What's your favorite movie?"

"This French movie called *Je Ne Sais Quoi*. It's amazing, you'd love it!"

Dan's eyebrows twisted.

"I'm kidding," she said. "Maybe, *Ever After*, or no, *Romy and Michele*. No! *Clueless!* Did you ever see that one? What's with the smile?"

"I've seen it, it's funny."

"It's your favorite!"

"I wouldn't go *that* far," He was really enjoying this, seeing this Annie again. He was glad she was still in there. "I do love that scene, though, when the dad yells at what's-her-name, *Get outta my chair!* And then the scene goes on as if nothing happened."

"Oh, so you *know* know this movie." A realization struck Annie. She gasped, "Have you watched it more than once?" Dan didn't say anything, he simply ran his tongue over his teeth, trying to stifle his growing grin. "*Oh em gee,* Dan, have you seen Clueless more than you've seen this movie?" She pointed at the screen.

Dan closed his eyes and sighed in defeat. Annie burst out a cackle before she could catch it—a laughter so sudden and severe it should have embarrassed her, but she didn't care. She grabbed Dan's arm and couldn't contain herself. It was the hardest he had ever seen her laugh. She tried to calm herself, but the laughter would escape out of her nose, or bounce in her throat with her tongue pinched between her teeth. She wiped a tear from her eye. "I knew it. I knew this movie was too boring—wait, who is he? Why does he look so familiar? The bald one, the creep."

"Telly Savalas? He was Kojak, that detective show from the seventies."

"No, that's not it. I never heard of that."

"He was in a Twilight Zone episode. That's all I can think of though."

"Oh, probably that. Which one?"

"The one with the little girl and that killer doll. Sort of like Chucky?"

"Thank you! Yes! I'm Talking Tina, and I'm going to kill you. Something like that, right? Good episode."

"I'm not your daddy!" The two of them laughed harder than the joke called for. Dan leaned in and kissed her head.

"God, I haven't seen that show in forever. I wish there was one of those New Year's Day marathons on right now. That would really hit the spot. I wonder why dads yelling at their kids is so funny sometimes," she said. "Here, hold my hand real quick." She put her hand in his, then leaned as far as she could across the bed, walking her fingers over to the remote, inching it finger by finger into her palm. Dan pulled her back into his arms and pointed the remote at the screen. "Do you mind if I change it?"

"Go ahead."

She stayed on the channel, "Hold up, he's handsome! My word. Who is he?"

"Cassavetes? He's actually a pretty famous director, but I think he started as an actor. He made these super realistic movies that didn't feel scripted. Artsy people go nuts over him. Real gritty stuff. So that guy there, the old one with the grey hair, he's a military guy and he has to take these prisoners and turn them into, like, a troop, I guess. But since they're all prisoners, they don't respond well to authority, but they eventually work together. Same ol' same ol'. But this guy is kind of anti-authority too, which is why he has this detail."

"You've seen this, then?" Annie said.

"Of course!" Dan waited a beat. "But just the one time." Annie did a little shimmy on the bed in victory, and Dan laughed, then continued. "There's a scene in the beginning where he's sitting in a room with all these officers that outrank him, and he's just talking back and not giving a fuck. I always liked it because he's the lowest guy in the room, like his rank—he's the one who has to salute everyone. But he controls the room as if he's the General. That, just, big, like, that swinging dick energy. I always wished I could do that—be the biggest man in the room even when I'm not. Because I never am."

She put her hand on his thigh and squeezed. "You're plenty big, babe."

Dan ran the back of his hand across his forehead, cartoonishly. "Phew!" He kissed the top of her head.

"So, that guy doesn't care at all? The cute one, he just does his own thing?" Annie said.

"Basically. If he doesn't do this job for the old man, then he's going to get hung, I think it was, or firing squad. One of those. And, if he does the job, he figures he'll probably get killed, suicide mission and all. So, he's like *Fuck it! I'm dead either way, why should I care about orders or rank?* What do they call that? Gallows humor?"

"Interesting," she said. "Death hangs over him, so it sets him free. Gives him all the power and makes him the big swinging dick." She nudged his side with her elbow.

"Is that part of the silver linings thing?"

"Take advantage of it while you can...I'm only on duty for the night. It's on you tomorrow." Annie turned her attention back to the TV, remote in her hand, but got distracted by the movie again.

Dan said, "Did you really not plan that stuff with the squirrels running across wires?"

"No, I swear," Annie said, her voice light with laughter. "It didn't even fit."

"We made it work, though."

"Yes, I did."

"Captain Video would be proud," Dan said, turning away from the TV to look at Annie.

"The Video Wizard!" Annie dropped the remote without changing the channel. She met Dan's gaze. "God, that's such a stupid name," she said, her voice airy, almost as if she was out of breath, inching her face closer to Dan's. A devilish smile on her face.

Dan kissed her and reached behind him, turning off the light, leaving only the glow from the TV and the sounds of war as they started to untie each other's robes.

15

IT WAS ANNIE'S IDEA FOR THEM TO GO FOR a walk. The day was hot, but not terrible, and it beat sitting in the car any longer, even with the A/C on. The smell worsened as the days went on, no matter how much they sprayed air freshener. They sat in the car at the drug store for forty-five minutes, but it seemed as eventful as the night before. That's when Annie had the idea to stretch their legs, and Dan agreed. It was between breakfast and lunch, and they had neither. Just a couple of cigarettes and some cans of beer that Annie was able to sweet-talk from the hard-headed guy at the gas station. The heat and the empty stomachs made the beer go right to their heads, which felt good until the heat and lack of water chipped away at them and chased all the light airy feelings from their minds. They popped into Allsup's, and Annie got a soft pretzel that was a few days old, and Dan a hot dog. They decided against more beer for now and each got a Gatorade instead.

"If we get out of this, no drinking, no cigarettes. Clean living," Dan said.

"We don't have to wait."

"No, I need them now," he laughed.

"You never told me your favorite movie," she said, ripping at her pretzel, her drink pinched between her body and elbow.

"What were the qualifications again? Comfort?"

"Comfort and rewatch...ability."

"So, a hangover movie, that's what I'm thinking. I only really watch movies when I'm on the couch or in bed feeling like shit. So, it needs to be mindless. And also on TV a lot, too."

"You're no fun at this," she said. "A hangover movie? How can that be a favorite?"

"Because it's comfortable and I watch it a lot."

Annie went to nudge him and dropped half her pretzel on the ground. Dan held onto his hot dog at the cost of getting ketchup on his hand.

"Boo, look what you made me do."

"Me?"

"Yes, you!"

"Five-second rule?" Dan said.

"Gross."

Dan gave her a bite of his hot dog, then finished the last bite, talking with his mouth full.

"Shawshank Redemption," Dan said. "It's on TV a lot and it's very long, even longer with commercials."

"But is it enjoyable?"

"In the sense that I enjoy not moving and staying under the covers when I'm hungover." Dan took a sip from his drink and stopped walking. Annie slowed to see what stopped him in his tracks. A beat-up Ford Taurus with dents and duct tape on the bumper, some tint peeling off the windows at the edges. And inside, about thirty scented pine trees hanging from every handle and mirror. They looked, but no one was around. Dan cupped his hands to the window and looked through his dark reflection. Fresheners in the vents and more trees hanging from the gear shift. New York license plates.

"It has to be," he said. "Right?"

"Why all the trees?"

He looked up and down the street. "I don't see anyone, do you?"

"No," she said. "There is a bench up the sidewalk, by that mailbox. Let's wait there."

The street stayed quiet. Some vehicles drove past, some people walked by, but no one stopped at the car. After a while, the sun shifted in the sky, and they were no longer in the shade, so Annie and Dan moved from their bench to a raised planter with a single tree in it. Annie kept wringing her hands, her leg bouncing more the longer they waited. Dan put his hand on her knee to settle it.

"I'm getting really nervous about this," she said. "I was excited about having a lead. And seeing all the air fresheners, I felt like maybe we're on to something but—" She looked at Dan, worry written all over her face. "Dan, what if this Rich guy killed her? What are we going to do?"

"I haven't thought that far ahead."

"What if he attacks us? Maybe we should just go."

"And do what? If this is the guy, we have to face him eventually." Dan thought for a moment. "Have you ever heard of that thing, that experiment with a cat in a box and, something like, there's a vial of poison in the box with them, but with the lid closed so there is no way to know if the poison killed the cat or not."

"That's horrible! I love cats! I'm glad that wasn't one of The Video Wizard's experiments," Annie said. "Good thing he just electrocuted stuffed squirrels."

"I don't know if it's true or just like a riddle or whatever, but the thing is that until the box is opened, the cat is both alive *and* dead at the same time—I think. I don't know the details, but it's what came to mind. And that's kind of the feeling I have. He *could be* dangerous, he could. And he could attack us and hurt us. *But*—"

"But Jackie already beats the shit out of us."

"Right. So, I'm already dead and alive at the same time, basically. With Jackie it's a sure thing, but this at least gives us some room. If I'm dead already, then I have more control than before. I never saw it that way until last night." He squeezed her knee again. "Jackie knows who you are, so I have to do everything I can think of to get us out of this. This is the only path I can see." Annie's leg slowed. "Plus, the tattoo guys didn't seem to be too scared of him, right? Maybe he didn't kill her, who knows. He tried to rob someone he already knew with a box cutter, so he's probably not all that dangerous. Or smart."

"Do we have any more cigarettes?"

"We smoked the last one when we first sat down."

"I'm going to go get us some," she said. "And some courage I can drink too. I'll be right back."

* * *

Almost as soon as Annie disappeared into the store, a man turned the corner, heading towards the car. Dan watched him closely. He sat as calm as he could, hiding his nervous energy and not exposing himself by shifting impatiently. Sitting with his elbows on his knees, looking at the ground between his feet, glancing up again, then back down, trying to appear casual. He didn't want to seem like he'd been waiting all day. When the man unlocked the door, Dan approached. Maybe he got up too fast. Maybe he was too aggressive. He spooked the guy but was able to hold his attention.

Over the man's shoulder, Dan saw Annie leave the store and stop dead when she saw he was talking to someone. He tried to signal to her not to approach without the man catching on.

The man was skinny with short hair. Trimmed nice on the sides and messy up top. Most importantly, he had a scar. Dan knew it was him. Somehow, in his gut, he just knew. Maybe you really could tell when people used to have dreadlocks. The man was jumpy and uncomfortable when Dan asked if his name was Rich—he nodded quickly, the color draining from his face, looking over his shoulder, chewing through his bottom lip, his hands fidgeting. Dan could see his skin leaking as the tension hung between them. It wasn't until Dan asked if he knew Lydia that Rich shoved him to the ground and took off running.

Dan was slow to get off the ground, scrambling to his feet and chasing after him. Annie dropped her bag, which came to life with a hiss, spraying beer on the ground, and ran after Dan—she called after him, and he yelled over his shoulder for her to stay there. Then the men were gone, and Annie reluctantly returned to the car, still partially opened. After quickly looking around, she sat down behind the wheel and closed the door behind her.

The smell in this car was putrid and more pungent than in Dan's car, even with all the trees hanging everywhere, adding layers and layers of linen, pine, and berries into the already awful mix. She lowered the sun visor like they do in the movies, expecting something to fall into her lap, but she didn't find anything. She opened the glove compartment and was surprised to find an actual pair of gloves. Besides that, there was just paperwork for the car, expired insurance cards, and registration. Richard Spector from New York, New York. The vehicle was dirty enough without the smell and the trees in it. Wrappers and napkins, crumpled bags of Dunkin' Donuts, empty paper cups. Crumbs.

Annie unfolded a piece of receipt paper. Double Mountain Motel and Restaurant. Room 257, paid for with cash. The rearview mirror was angled sharply downward, showing the backseat instead of the rear window. Annie turned around. The rear seat on the passenger side was stained a dark maroon, long strands of hair lying in the red. She was hesitant to do it, but she touched the stain. The fabric was stiff. Annie tried to lift one of the hairs from the seat, but it was cemented in place.

The knock on the window made her scream and grab the handle, clutching it closed.

"Come on, let's go," Dan said.

"Where's Richard?" she said through the window, releasing her grip.

"He got away, come on, let's go. My hand's killing

me." Dan opened the door and helped her out of the car. She told him about the motel receipt and the stain.

"I doubt he's going back there right away," he said. Dan took the phone out of his pocket. "What is this shit? I can't find anything on here. I want my fucking phone back."

"What are you doing?" Annie picked up the soggy brown bag and cans from the street and carried them until they got to the first garbage they found on their way back to the drug store.

"I'm calling Jackie. Fuck that guy. *My goddamn hand*."

"We can't tell Jackie yet," she said. "We don't know anything." She took the phone from him. "Dan, you know what he'll do to whoever we find. We have to be sure."

Dan screamed in frustration, then calmed down as much as he could. "I need a new brace. This one doesn't do shit. It broke when he shoved me. How the fuck did I get us tangled up in this?"

"Nope," Dan said, chewing two more aspirins then washing them down with his beer. The two of them sat on the balcony of their hotel room, and Annie passed her cigarette back to him. "As soon as I asked about Lydia, he knocked me over and took off. Nothing else."

"I was hoping there was more. That maybe after your hand stopped hurting as much and we showered and things calmed down that you might remember some other detail. Anything."

"That's all there was to it."

"It makes sense then, why he was so nervous when you approached him. He's probably just waiting for what's coming his way."

"But what is coming? Why stick around? His car isn't exactly low key with all that shit. I guess the tints help, but it's still a risk." The sun started to sink lower in the sky, an evening glow of pink and orange peeked through the buildings and filled in all the empty spaces between. "What's his angle?"

Annie took the cigarette back. "Maybe there is no angle," she said, her voice slightly higher from holding in a lung full of smoke. She exhaled. "Maybe he's just not that bright? Or maybe he's strung out?"

He took one last drag, looked at the butt in his hand, then flicked it over the balcony. "Speaking of which, I wish we had something. Some weed or something. That'd be nice. Fuck all this anxiety, just waiting for the sky to fall on us."

"Or the ground from underneath us. That's how we'll celebrate when it's all done," Annie said.

"Deal. Are you ready to head out?"

"As ready as I'll ever be."

16

THE DOUBLE MOUNTAIN MOTEL AND Restaurant was old and only lived up to half its name. The restaurant had been closed for almost a decade, and the brown discolored windows of the sunroom were an ugly reminder of a dining area that was probably designed in the late 70s and never updated. The rooms wrapped around the courtyard of the place, the cement a pale green, painted a darker shade at one time, now bleached from the sun. A shallow swimming pool sat in the center, and the water was cleaner than Dan expected. He figured it'd be empty or maybe a murky dark color with something like an abandoned tricycle in it, based on the rest of the place. Rich's car was parked in the lot, in the corner, far from the other cars.

Dan and Annie looked at each other, their faces somber and nervous. A mix of understanding that they were passing the point of no return, with no power to stop it. The roller coaster was at the top of its climb—stalling for that brief moment before gravity caught it and did its thing. And, in that quiet instant, before the drop, it was as peaceful as anything would ever be again. The wind gusted and blew past them with a rush, and they were back in motion, heading up the stairs that wrapped around the pool to the second floor. Dan shook the energy from his fingers as he walked, trying to kick the last of the nerves pulsating from his stomach and down his limbs, tingling his hands and numbing his feet.

Room 257.

Dan knocked, and after a moment, the door peeked open as far as the chain would allow. Before any words were exchanged, the door was slammed, and there was a commotion on the other side—the sounds of furniture being flipped. Dan started banging on the door, telling Rich to open up. Then a thud and the crash of broken glass.

"Oh God, he's going to jump," Annie said and ran down the stairs. Dan rammed his shoulder into the door. And again. A small, almost painless, pop came from the top of his shoulder. Dan grimaced, and rammed the door again, before the door jamb splintered, pulling the top hinge from the wall.

"Don't jump," Dan said, running in as he watched Rich disappear out the window. "No!" A brief silence, then a sharp scream followed by a long guttural moan. Dan looked out the broken window and saw Rich rolling on the ground, grabbing his shin. Annie stood next to him, looking between him and Dan.

"I didn't kill her," Rich said as he rolled on the ground. "*My fucking leg.*" He let out a grunt and repeated over and over again how he didn't kill Lydia. Dan scrambled down the stairs, expecting to see nosy neighbors looking out their windows, but all the curtains were drawn tight. Dan grabbed the chair Rich threw out the window and walked toward him.

"Stop," Rich said. "Don't do whatever you're about to."

"Calm down, kid, I'm just giving you a place to sit."

"I don't trust you, stay away."

Rich tried to stand. Something snapped loudly and Rich fell over with a yelp—his leg bending in the wrong direction. His eyes shot open, and three short gasps of air hissed out before he registered to scream.

"We have to get him to the hospital," Annie said.

"You know, for a moment, I forgot how close to the ground we were. I thought he killed himself," Dan said, then started laughing. Annie smacked his arm. The two of them sat in the car in the hospital parking lot, waiting for Rich. They had already been there for over an hour. The car ride to the hospital was filled with Rich moaning and grunting in the back seat, repeating his innocence. When they first loaded him back there, Annie instinctively apologized for the smell—in hindsight, it was a wasted gesture.

"I don't think he did it," Annie said.

"I don't think so either, but he knows something to jump like that."

"Poor guy."

"I wouldn't go that far. He's still involved somehow."

"So are we," Annie said. "I can't help but see how much pain he's in."

"That break was nasty. Something you only see in a UFC fight or, like, football."

"I don't mean his leg. He just seems to be hurting, you know," she said and tapped her chest with her fingertips, "from the inside out." They smoked two cigarettes each and listened to music on the radio, sometimes singing, sometimes sitting silently. A nurse appeared at the entrance of the Emergency Room, wheeling out Rich in a chair, his leg in a cast. The nurse gave Annie a copy of his papers and some prescriptions for pain killers that still needed to be filled. Rich slept the whole ride.

It was a production to get Rich back up the stairs to his room, the door busted and mostly open. They draped an arm over each shoulder and tried to get Rich to hop on his good foot, but he was too drugged and dopey, so Dan just ended up carrying him. They had no way of telling if anything of his was stolen. The cold night air filled his room through the broken window. They scanned the scene and laid Rich on one of the two beds. Dan nodded his head toward the door, and they moved a dresser to keep it closed.

"Now what?" Annie said.

"I guess we wait for him to wake up. Why don't you use that bed? I'll stay awake," Dan said. "He seems pretty harmless, especially in this state, but even so, one of us should stay up."

"Too much excitement, I probably won't be able to sleep," she said.

Dan popped on the TV and turned the volume low. "I would at least try. I'll wake you up when I start to drift."

Rich woke in the morning, the bright sun stabbing his eyes through the curtains that were billowing in the breeze of the broken window. Dan and Annie were sitting at the table eating breakfast. Dan pushed a greasy white bag to the empty spot on the table.

"Breakfast," he said through a mouthful, continuing to eating. Rich hesitantly sat with them. His movement was awkward, thudding unsteadily with each step, his cast heavy on the floor.

"How are you feeling?" Annie said.

"Like dog shit run over twice," Rich said. Dan started laughing. "What's so funny?"

"Your accent. The New York of it. Dog, D A W G."

Rich chuckled at the impression and ravenously attacked his breakfast sandwich. He swallowed his bite and took another one. "Who are you guys?" Crumbs falling from his mouth.

"Just two people who seem to be in as deep over their heads as you are," Dan said.

"You two look like shit, no offense."

"Yeah, it hasn't been a picnic," Dan said.

"Finding you wasn't easy," Annie said. She held her hand over her mouth as she talked, hiding the remaining food in her mouth.

"Why were you looking for me? I mean, I know why," he said. His face turned red, and his eyes filled with water, the brief quiver in his chin betraying him. "How do you know Lydia?"

"We don't," Dan's voice stifled from speaking mid-swallow. "Do you know who Lydia's dad is?"

"Yeah, I know of him. He's a real piece of shit, right? I never met him."

"A piece of shit, but he's very powerful," Dan said.

"And dangerous," Annie said.

"Very," Dan said. "He's the one looking for you."

"He knows about me? About what happened?" Rich said. His eyes grew wider, more worry painting his face.

"He doesn't know you exist, but he's looking for you all the same," Dan said.

"Jackie is making us track down whoever killed his daughter," Annie said. She balled up the wrapper of her sandwich and tossed it in the bigger bag on the table.

"But," Rich said, defensive and riddled with panic, "I didn't kill her. I would never." He cleared his throat. "Did he do that to you?"

"Him and his guys, yeah." Dan wiped his mouth with his napkin. "It's not been pleasant."

"Are you going to, you know, turn me in? To her dad?"

"I'm not sure I have a choice, kid. I'm sorry," Dan said. Rich put his head down on the table, crying. Messy sobs, hiccuping breaths.

"Please don't call me kid," Rich said, softly, almost a plea. Dan apologized.

"Rich," Annie said, and touched his arm. "You said you didn't kill her?"

"I didn't," he tried to calm his breathing. "I swear I didn't." A strange calmness came over him. "Maybe you should."

"Should what? Turn you over to Jackie?" Annie said.

"It's for the best. I can't go on like this. I didn't kill her, really. But I'm the reason she's dead. It's my fault. What the fuck does it matter? Just have him put me out of my misery! I'm a fuck up anyway, not like anyone would give a shit." He took a deep breath, closed his eyes, then put his hands flat on the table, calm and collected. "Okay, let's go."

Confusion shot between Annie and Dan. "Let's

not jump to that just yet. Why don't you tell us what happened?" Dan said.

Rich stood up and limped over to the corner of the room. He tried to reach a ceiling panel.

"Could you give me a hand?"

Dan walked over and poked at the ceiling. It had a weight to it. He lifted the next panel and slid it out of the way, fishing around with his hand. He felt something. Leather and heavy. He gave Rich a confused look and pulled down the satchel from the ceiling. Rich limped over and opened the case. It was packed to the brim with cash. Stacks and stacks of money. All wrapped up in bundles, mostly one-hundred-dollar bills.

"What the fuck is this?"

"A little less than seventy-five grand," Rich said.

Dan slumped back into his chair, his eyes bulging from his head, shaking back and forth with confusion.

"Okay," Dan said. "What the fuck is going on?"

17

"ME AND LYDIA ONLY DATED A FEW months before we moved to New York, we were both stuck, and she hated her old man."

"Who doesn't," Dan said.

"Things we're good, but not great. I'm always broke. I was never any good with money, but I knew I could survive back in New York. Better than here. I know they say that shit about *if you can make it here,* but it was always just easier for me to make it back there. I was broke, but she had some scratch saved up. And it held us over for a while. We probably should have gotten an apartment, maybe, the money could have lasted longer. We never liked the idea of being tied down—we didn't even stay at the same motel for more than a few weeks. At first, when things were better than good, we had money, and we were in love. If not love, the closest we could be to it. Our biggest mistake was that we should have been working the whole time and not living off the money. We were shoveling money away faster than we refilled it. Always the common thread in almost every break-up story. Money problems."

"You two broke up?" Annie said.

"No, but it was close. We loved each other too much to walk away. But we'd fight and I'd leave for a bit. I'd come home, and we'd work on it, then repeat."

"Where would you go when you left?" Annie said.

"Another motel, a friend, sometimes there was—sometimes there were other women. Maybe she knew, I don't know, but the cool down was good for us."

"What happened when the money ran out?" Dan looked at the satchel and then at Annie. It took her a moment, and she flinched.

"Is that her money? Did you? Then steal her—" she said.

"I didn't kill her, I told you," Rich said, tired and frustrated at repeating himself.

"Sorry. Go on," Annie said.

"When the money ran out, we got jobs. What else could we do? I got a job working at a pool hall, but no one plays pool anymore, so I just tended bar at a place with a lot of pool tables. Lydia got a job at a coffee shop. Like a hipster one, in a rich part of the city. The kind that spell shop *shoppe*. She had a unique look to her, with all the black work and face stuff, so it wasn't too easy for her to get a job—but that place ate it up. Even with full-time hours for her and part-time for me, the money wasn't enough. Band-Aids on a bullet wound. The fighting increased, and the sex decreased. We did have something, though. Whatever it was between us that kept us going, even if we didn't tell each other we loved 'em, it was there."

Rich would zone out, lost in the kaleidoscoped memories, and without knowing it, his face would show all the emotions of all the thoughts he retraced in his head. Then he'd snap out of it and continue. "The coffee shoppe, right. So, she's working, and since the day she started, one of the regulars started giving her a hard time. A real fucking son of a bitch. Some stockbroker—suits everyday, briefcase, wallet he kept in the inside pocket of his jacket—you know the guy. Older, not like old old, late fifties. Fifty-eight, actually. At least that's what the news said."

"The news?" Annie said.

Rich hesitated, "He's dead."

"The Wall Street guy? We've seen stories," Dan said.

Annie said, "We never paid attention. That's the guy?"

"I can't believe that made it all the way out here. People die every day in the city, like *every fucking day*, and this guy is a national story? But he was a big shot, I guess. We had no idea. To Lydia, he was just that asshole who talked down to her. Snide comments here and there about her looks, or that negging shit people do when they think they are a lady's man—saying stuff like *You'd be pretty if you didn't look how you do*, then some bullshit about her mod work. Shitting on her with one sentence, then trying to fuck her with the next."

Annie scoffed, "It's amazing what guys think works."

"Sometimes he'd leave her like a fifty-dollar tip on some seven-dollar coffee that he paid for with a credit card. Throw money at everything and everyone, and eventually you'll get the girl you look down on to blow you. Then you can go high-five your Wall Street dick-heads with their stupid Bluetooth hanging from their ear.

He was a real creature of habit, too—same drink, same time, every morning, Monday through Friday.

"Lydia did her best to avoid him—going in the back, restocking cups, anything not to have to deal with this fucking guy when he came in. She'd come home after work and complain about her day. Even when things weren't great, I would listen. After months of these stories, I really started to hate him, too. I was no saint, I fucked around, I admit that, but I still hated to see her so upset. One day, it was just too much for her. Maybe she was agitated at me, or maybe she didn't sleep that well, or shit, maybe she just had enough—I really don't know—but as she's handing him his drink, he makes some crack about her, something real shitty. He grabs her hand and goes *How are you ever going to get me to cum on those tits if you never smile at me, sweetheart?*"

"I hope she threw that drink in his face." Annie's face was trembling with rage. "I hope it was hot, too. Scolding."

"Not even," Rich said. "She took the drink back before he could grab it and threw it out. That was it. And, she told him to go fuck himself...and ripped up his money. But of course, what does he do?"

"Gets her fired," Dan said.

"Yup. *Do you know who I am?!* Blah blah blah. We knew we had enough money to survive while she found a new job, except—"

"She couldn't find one?" Annie said.

"For weeks, she looked. Other coffee places, liquor stores. *Fucking. Tattoo. Shops.*" His disbelief and annoyance showed in how he emphasized each syllable like typewriter strikes. "Nothing. I'm not sure why she didn't want to go to her mom, but she didn't. And she obviously didn't want to go to her old man. That was a non-starter. She hated him. Which is easy enough to do."

"Yes, it is," Dan said. Rich carried on, barely registering the interjection.

"So, we're drinking, and talking, and venting. Doing lines of coke. It's a real bad situation."

"Coke?" Annie said.

"The money runs out real fast when you're dumb, but I've never had a bad idea when I'm ripped, you know how it is. And we just kept going back to that guy, that fucking guy. Isaac Charles. It's all him. He broke her. He got her fired. I got this idea. Me and my fucking plans. Especially in that state. An idea to get money from him. It was weeks later, and I'm sure he'd forgotten about her. He probably never thought about her again. For us, it broke us in half and left us scrambling—we were drowning—but for him, it was a regular Wednesday. No one's going to remember one girl he yelled at in a coffee shop months ago, you know?"

"What was the plan?" Dan said.

"It was simple, too simple, I thought. He's an asshole, right? And the way he talked to Lydia wasn't new to him. It was safe to assume that is just who he is, to everyone, especially women. We got a burner phone, like the disposable ones from 7-11, and after some searching, we were able to figure out how to contact him. Google, LinkedIn, Facebook, all that shit. Lydia could find Waldo in a candy cane factory when it came to social media. We called up and threatened to come clean about what he did to that girl."

"Lydia? Or was there another girl, too? What did he do?" Annie said.

"We had no idea. We just said it. That's the thing, though, right? That was our thinking—if someone has a lot of money and power and treats everyone like trash, like they own them and shit, of course they'll have any number of stories that fit that description. She'd always have stories about her old man's paranoia, how exhausting it was to deal with. *We know what you did to that girl.* Keep it simple. Vague. Always vague. People like that are always suspicious, their always on guard. Enemies closer, type shit. Always assuming someone's trying to screw them. We figured, let them fill in the gaps, use their own paranoia against them."

"He didn't have any follow-up questions? He just took you at your word?" Dan said.

"Their suspicions being correct is the only thing fucks like them don't question. They're the smartest in the room. Whenever he'd ask us anything, we'd say shit like *Don't try to be cute, you know damn well who.* And when he'd try to call your bluff, we'd just pile on more vagueness. *That picture on your phone, yes that photo. We have it and we'll send it to everyone in your address book. Your phone number is still,* and then we'd just say his number back to him. He'd get so nervous that he didn't even realize we had his number because we called *him*. People like that, I don't know, privilege makes you a special kind of dumb. He assumed we hacked his account. Or we'd describe some random photo from his Facebook, a real deep dive. We figured he didn't know too much about technology. He still used a Bluetooth earpiece, not even a nice one or an earbud, it was those old ones that clamped over his ear. Ridiculous. And his age and wealth—plus he's white—so he's probably scared of getting canceled or *Me Too*ed. You stay with it long enough, then pretty soon the person isn't doing anything except freaking out. But you gotta keep it simple. And vague. We got a voice scrambler, some cheap bullshit thing from Amazon. The distorted voice does a lot of the heavy lifting. At least it did with him."

"Maybe he'd been scared of being found out for a while," Annie said.

"Then you call and it's his worst nightmare come to life," Dan said.

"Simple and vague." The excitement in his voice was gone, and it got thick, cracking as he trailed off. "It was supposed to be simple at least." Rich fought through the memory, cleared his throat, and shook his head quickly, snapping back to focus. "Eighty grand. To keep us quiet, bring eighty grand in cash to this location. Some abandoned lot in Queens—get him to some place he wouldn't be comfortable—we did the whole *come alone* bullshit. If we see anyone, we're releasing the picture.

"I should have been the one to confront him. But she wanted to. She wanted to see him scared, watch him tremble. Squirm. It was personal for her. It was my plan, and I let her meet him...and I was too far away to do anything about it. We wore masks, you know, ski masks. I knew how much she wanted him to see it was her, but we promised we'd do it right. Totally covered up. No faces, no visible tattoos, no piercings showing, nothing. I was behind one of those shipping containers, the big metal kind, I had a clear view. He came alone, with the bag, this one. We were doing it, we were pulling it off."

"You didn't bring any sort of protection?" Annie said.

"The finger gun in the pocket was too much of a

giveaway, we thought. It would show our bluff. She had a box cutter just in case, but that was all we brought. She had it in her hand too, to scare him. He placed the bag between them. And when she went to grab it...he reached into his jacket and pulled out a piece of pipe, like this." He held his hands out about eight inches from each other, palm to palm. He stopped talking and looked at the space between his hands, staring. His chin quivered. "And he just, fucking—" He pantomimed swinging the pipe three times. He took a deep breath. "Before I knew what happened, he was beating her. I can still hear the sound. I ran as fast as I ever ran. Everything was shapeless. Sounds were blurred. But before I could get to him, she fell over. She didn't even catch herself, just fell over and hit her face on the cement. He was stomping on her, and she was...just lying there. No defense, no movement."

Annie covered her mouth, and Dan gently squeezed her leg.

"I tackled him, and the pipe went flying. I was just punching him over and over and over." He repeated over and over under his breath. *Over and over.* "He was moaning, I remember that. I picked his head up by his hair and just—" Again, he pantomimed driving the head into the ground. "His breathing was funny. It was wet. He was gasping.

"When I got over to Lydia, she was already gone, man. I could just tell. I tried to lift her and..." Clearing his throat once didn't do the trick, so he went again. "She was the heaviest thing I've ever felt. Her eyes were glassy—but it was different, you could almost see those, I don't know, something floating in the glaze. I've never seen that before. I tried to listen for a heartbeat, there was nothing. Not in her chest or her wrist or her neck. Nothing. She was gone, I just knew it. It's like I knew it from the first hit of the pipe." His tears broke over his cheeks when he said how he hoped she didn't suffer. "*I really hope she didn't.*" He stopped talking and stared off into the corner of the room. Looking at nothing. "I heard that, that, wet, that fucking wet breathing coming from the guy, you know? Gurgling. So, I got his pipe in my hand, I walked over and—I don't even know. But he was deader than Lydia when I finished."

"That's horrible," Annie said. "I don't know what—that's...it's horrible."

"It was my fault. She'd still be alive if she had never met me," Rich said. He tried to keep his breathing under control.

"But her body," Annie said. "We saw it just a few hours from here."

"You saw her?" Rich broke down and cried. He put his head on the table and let it all come sobbing out. His breathing was fast and irregular—big gasps of panicked breaths—then more crying. He picked his head up and closed his eyes, breathing slowly through his nose and out of his mouth.

"That's right, bud, just breathe, it's alright," Dan said. "Take your time." Rich had one last outburst of crying, then breathed sharply out of his mouth before calming down.

"Before we left for New York, back when were here, still fresh, in the honeymoon of things—" His mind drifted. "I'm not sure what she ever saw in me, but I was too afraid to ask. Scared it would make her realize something I didn't want her to realize. Because, man, I really did love her. I know that now. And I wish I knew it then. *I'm so fucking stupid.* All the time I am, all the time. Sorry.

"Before New York, we dated for a few weeks here. Honeymoon stuff. *Everything-was-great-and-nothing-hurt* type of relationship. We couldn't get enough of each other, hanging out every day, all day. Sex all the time—shower, pulling over when we drove—we really couldn't stay off of each other. And one day she said she wanted to show me something. One of those special things she regretted showing others. She drove me to this place up north by T or C—her little secret. I mean, that's how much she loves it. Fuck. Loved it, how much she loved it. She would say things like that, like, *I brought so and so here, and I regret wasting the memory.* It made sense to me, though. We all have that. We share our favorite song with someone, then they do something, that's what she meant. And I was glad she showed it to me. She thought she swore off sharing that place forever.

"We went up there a few times together, but that first time...that first time was perfect. We made good time, too. Not travel time, but time of day—the sun was setting on the drive as we got close. Then we got to the top of the trail and there were all these reds and pinks in the sky—patches of orange—I'll always remember that. I wish I paid more attention. Just sat in the moment, you know? These things don't hit everyone equally, now I have all these regrets. Was I too short? Did I show enough thanks for sharing it?" Rich stopped talking, his memory staring a hole through the table.

"—The sky was pink and red and orange, and you

could see the silhouette of the cliffs. You could still make them out a little bit, they almost looked purple. And she told me when she died, she wanted to be buried there. She said she wished there was a tree, that was the only thing she cared about. She wanted a tree to be buried under. She talked about planting one, maybe—then, when she was old and it was grown, she'd have a tree to lie under. There wasn't a tree, but what else could I do? I couldn't leave her in Queens or have the ambulance come and just, I dunno, take her away."

"You drove her from New York all the way across the country, to here?" Dan said.

Annie's voice came out in a whisper, "That's so far."

"I didn't know what else to do. I was scared. I was beside myself. I took the bag of money and drove her back home. Back to where she wanted to lie forever. I am going to—I was going to—plant a tree there. So, it'd grow for her. I just needed to wait until, I mean, I just was scared to see her. I was waiting."

"This is the ransom money, then?" Dan said.

"I'm too scared to spend it," Rich said. "It takes me forever to break the bills down. I don't know if they are traced or anything. I try to find ways to avoid using it until I break them into something smaller. Not that it matters. I'm ready when you are."

Dan sat, looking at the broken door of the hotel, the splintered hinges, and the furniture holding it closed. "Look ki—Rich, this is a lot to process. Let's stick a pin in the Jackie shit for tonight. We have all this new information, and we need to think on it. If we leave you here, are you going to run off on us?"

Rich framed the sides of his cast with his hands.

"Where am I going to go?" He puffed a sharp chuckle, talking to himself under his breath. *Run off.*

"All the same, give us your keys. And give us your number, we'll be in touch. Just lay low, and...Rich, be smart."

Dan stood up, and Annie followed suit, her eyes bulging the tiniest bit in nonverbal communication—things just got impossibly harder for them. Dan returned her look, and they headed for the door. Dan's hand gently guiding Annie by the small of her back. He stopped and turned to Rich, almost shyly.

"Would you happen to know where we could get some weed?"

18

DAN AND ANNIE STOOD ON THE BALCONY of their hotel room with their heads floating above them on strings. Rich gave them a joint he rolled a day earlier, unable to smoke it because the two of them knocked on his door. Dan figured, based on how the room smelled, that he stood a good chance if he asked. *It kicks like a mule,* Rich said when he handed it over. Dan and Annie smoked the joint, watching the day turn into night—passing it back and forth between each other.

"What are you thinking?" Annie said through a cloud of smoke before the wind pushed it from the balcony.

"I'm not sure," Dan said, holding in his cough, chin tucked to his chest to keep it from escaping. "Jackie is going to kill him, we both know that. It doesn't matter the technicality of shit and who killed who. He's going to kill that kid."

"It probably won't be fast either."

"I doubt it would be. So," Dan handed the joint back

to Annie. "What does that mean for us? We'd be killing him if we handed him over."

"I don't think we should," Annie said. "How could we live with ourselves if we let...*that* happen to him?"

"He's hurting, you can see that. And he acts like he's ready to die, but I don't know."

"He jumped out the window to try and escape."

"Do you do that if you're ready to die?"

She passed the butt to Dan again, surrounded by the earthy skunk that burned from the paper. Dan continued, "It's just—we're dead if we don't turn him over. Or if we say we couldn't find anyone. I'm not willing to let you die in his place."

"I don't want to die, Dan." Her voice cracked.

"This is starting to go to my head. I can't focus right now. Let's lie down."

Floating in bed, Dan looked at the ceiling—at the shadows and the small holes that spread across the tiles. Annie lay next to him, her head on his chest, after it caught up from lagging behind on the balcony.

"Do you think that was just pot?" Dan said.

"Are we getting old?"

"What?"

"You called it pot," Annie said, laughing. "Only old people call it pot."

"Sorry. Do you think that was just weed?"

"Doesn't feel like it."

"I'm not complaining," Dan said.

"Me neither." Annie took a few slow breaths. Dan thought for a moment she might have fallen asleep. Her voice pierced the silent haze. "Do you remember the first time you ever smoked pot?"

"Not really. Sometimes I feel like I should smoke more, it'd be easier on my liver," said Dan, a chuckle punctuating his own joke. Annie shook, but was too relaxed to make a sound. "Whenever I'm stoned, it takes me forever to do anything. My PEMDAS gets all out of whack. It'll take me five minutes to open a beer because I'll think it's a better idea to take out the bottle, then the church key, then turn on the TV so it's ready by the time I sit down, then I'll open the beer, and I'll, like, throw out the top, which I never do any other time—instead of...just sitting down and cracking a beer."

Annie was vibrating with giggles, wiping a tear from her eye. "*My PEMDAS*, I can't."

"I always overthink everything, my whole order of operations."

"I know, I just hate how much I get what you mean. You're *so* stupid." Her words were lost through her laughter and Dan watched as her head bounced as his stomach contracted with each chuckle, which made Annie laugh harder, which would take Dan deeper into his own fit, which shook her head more. They might never stop.

It finally died down to sporadic bouts of trying to contain it, and Dan continued, slightly more somber. "We should do this more."

"I'd like that. This is so nice. Can you rub my back?"

"This has to be better than drinking, right?"

"I never took the time to compare them," she said. The two lay quietly. Motionless, with their thoughts ringing in their ears.

"Why'd I start talking about this? Did you ask me something?"

A burst of air shot from Annie's nose with a snort.

"If you remembered the first time you smoked pot." This threw them into another fit of stifled laughter.

"I was probably drunk, if I had to guess." Dan faded into thought. "I remember having my first beer though," he said. "It was at a party the captain of the Track Team threw after winning some big race, probably Counties or something. Oh shit—"

"What?"

"I had my first beer with Jackie."

Dan expected her head to shoot up exaggeratedly, but she kept her cheek on his chest. "Really?" she said, her voice wispy and listless.

"Not with him. He was on the team, so he would have been there."

"Imagine he gave you your first beer? That'd be crazy."

"If he set this whole mess in motion."

"You're not a mess, hun," she said. "I remember the first time I smoked pot. Me and my girlfriend—Oh my god, I am old. My girlfriend? Who am I, my grandma? She says that about her female friends. Sorry, me and my best friend, we got some weed from a kid at school and smoked it in her basement. We didn't know, we thought it would be like drinking, so we wrote down all our great ideas, thinking we'd forget them, like we'd black out or something. Silly things, like buying fruit for the next time we smoked or a funny movie to watch. But you just, like, remember everything. Yeah, I don't think this is just pot. It feels nice. Can you turn the light off? But only if you can reach without moving."

Dan didn't even attempt it, he dropped his arm to the side of the bed and tugged the cord from the wall.

Annie wanted to listen to music, the dark room punctuated by the blue glow of her phone as she scrolled. She pressed the screen and placed her phone face down on the bed. The song that poured out rippled over the bed—synthetic and layered, electronic chimes, calming like the slow crawl of water back to the sea.

The smoke stayed on the balcony, but the drugs continued to pump through his blood, and Dan closed his eyes. The sounds of the song turned into waves he watched spread throughout the room. Rippling too fast to see—only the blur of movement. He lost his surroundings and became something other than who he was moments ago. His body had no structure, changing him into the vibrations of music. He couldn't feel his limbs—they all merged when his body turned into echoes of sound. His mind zoomed into his new form and found another world within, nesting inside each other. His body contained the whole universe.

He zoomed into that world and found another. Microscopic but bigger than him. Everything was a world within itself. And Dan saw that everything had a center. And all the centers were connected. Annie's head was no longer lying on his chest, but it was his chest. The vibrations rippling through her head fell into the empty spaces of his shoulder until she was absorbed, and they were one. Dan fell deeper into the darkness of his mind, an endless blackness. But he wasn't scared. It wasn't an abyss—just infinity. And he floated. Weightless. Swimming through the shapeless void. He felt as if he were both falling and flying. Then the ceiling was gone, leaving only the sky. And he saw Annie's head on his chest as he lay on the bed, thinking the thoughts he was watching unfold. Warm air crawled over his chest, and her breathing got deeper, and his did too. He was sleeping and awake. He was her, and she was him, and they were the atoms and the particles that made up the atoms. They were the vibrations and the blur of their movement. The time between seconds.

Dan thought of all the things he felt and everything he feared. He realized that love felt the same to him as it did to others. To Annie. To Trevor. Even Jackie. Hurt and loss, too. Everyone was connected, and everyone was the same—the rest were details. He thought of Lydia and how it must feel to lose a daughter, and he thought of his dad and everything he felt after he died. That was a heart attack, this is murder. And Dan thought of everyone he was scared of losing to Jackie. He wondered if Jackie reflected on himself as a dad, as a person, the things he did, what he said or should have said, or did he bury it all down into rage. He almost felt for Jackie, understanding him so deeply in that moment, his empathy expanding beyond anything he knew. But he hated Jackie and didn't want to think of him anymore, so he returned to his present. He couldn't place this feeling, and he wondered if maybe it was God, moving through his blood like oxygen. And if it was God, could it deliver him safely if a snake clung to his face? He didn't know, but he felt peaceful. He was Annie, and she was him. And it finally occurred to Dan what the feeling was, and why he didn't recognize it—he never felt happiness like this before, and he was desperate to keep it.

Then he was asleep.

Dan dreamt of fishing with his father on a lake he couldn't picture but still saw clearly. His dad was explaining how the different lures worked—the twitches and movements needed to make them look real. Telling him that if his timing was off, then it was all over, and any chance for success would be gone. Dan would always tug the rod too soon. His dad's voice sounded like Rich. *No, patience. Wait. Make it look real. The fish has to believe it. Become what it's expecting to see. Lull it, become its projection. Gentle, slow, reel. Wait. Then again. When the timing is right—Remember, son, the bait is fake. Make the fish think the trick is real. The fish's mind does the bulk of the work, always remember that.*

Then the sun melted into the sea, and the water swallowed his dad and changed him into a liquid darkness. No figure. And everything went black—the lake and New York mountains faded, and the water turned red like blood, then the blood into rust-colored sand. A grey street slithered its curves through the flat sand. And Dan walked by himself, the heat making the horizon dance like a mirage, disappearing into a point.

When Annie woke, she was alone in bed with no sign of Dan.

19

IT TOOK A MOMENT AFTER DAN KNOCKED before he heard any movement. Then the thumping of the dresser. *Thump, grunt, thump grunt.* The door opened a few inches, and Rich peeked out.

"You have to answer me something and answer it honestly," Dan said. "If I let you go, are you going to waste it? I don't want to do what I'm about to, and then it turns out you're coked out of your mind down in Mexico or some shit. Wasting sixty-five grand on drugs and alcohol and going back to your schemes."

"Sixty-five grand?"

"Just answer the question."

"I won't waste it."

"Promise me that."

"I promise."

"And you'll get out of town today?"

"Today. I'll just drive—"

"Don't tell me. Don't tell me anything, just go."

"Okay, I will. I promise."

"You promise?"

"Fuck man, yeah I promise."

"That's three. Don't go back on it. Here are your keys." Dan paused and cleared his throat. "I'm going to need some money."

20

THE PHONE ONLY RANG ONCE BEFORE Annie picked up.

"Where are you?" She said.

Dan was outside Jackie's place, calling from the cell phone he gave him, stomach in knots, thinking about the last time he was here. Thinking about what was about to happen. He walked around to the back of the building across the street and crouched next to some dry shrubs—wanting to stay out of sight as long as he could so Jackie, or one of his asshole thugs, couldn't interrupt if they saw him from a window. The air was still, and the sun beat down relentlessly on the back of his neck.

"If I could get us out of this," Dan said. "Truly get us out of this, for good. Do you think we could make a go of it? Me and you? If we weren't tied together by this. Were you serious about the stuff you said?"

"Dan." The pause stretched on just short of an eternity. "What are you about to do?"

"Please, Annie. I need to know."

“Dan, of course I’m serious, I always was. You’re scaring me.”

“What about Trevor? What if he wants you back?”

“You’re talking so fast.”

“I just need to know. Can we really make a go of it?”

“We’ll make a go of it, yes. I’ll have to figure out Trevor, I can’t avoid that—but I was serious, Dan. About everything.”

The wind blew a faint whistle through the silence.

“Me and you, right? Till the end of the line.”

“Until the end,” Annie said. “Hun, come get me and we’ll figure out what to do.”

“I think I figured it out. Talking to Richard last night gave me an idea. I just needed to make sure. In case.”

“And when we’re done, no more drinking!”

“Except to celebrate.”

“Yes, but then no more after that.” Annie thought for a beat. “Well, less. Let’s not go crazy.”

“Exactly, no more crazy.”

“Dan...you’re about to do something crazy, though, aren’t you?”

“Yes. But it’s the last time.”

“What are you about to do?”

“Probably the dumbest thing I’ve ever done. But it’s the only play we have. It’ll work, it will.”

“I believe you, Dan. Be careful and come home to me.”

“It’ll take a miracle, but—it has to work. It will. It will.” He sat listening to the wind blow. “I didn’t mean for this to be the first time I say it to you—but I love you. Remember that.”

“Come home to me and tell me again when we’re

together. When this is all done, and we can just leave, we'll keep driving. Like we said."

"Just like we said."

"I've still never been to Spain," she said. "That's far away. I'd like that."

"That's more than a car ride," he said.

"That's okay. Do you know what kind of fishing they have there?"

"I'm not sure."

"Me neither, so come home and we can find out." Her voice softened even more. "And Dan," she said.

"Yeah?"

"Vaya con Dios."

The smile grew so large across his face that he was sure Annie could hear it on the other side.

"In a while, crocodile."

Dan hung up the phone and slouched against the brick wall behind him. He held the phone in his hands like a prayer and gently tapped it against his forehead, trying to muster the courage to get up. He checked his back pocket nervously, feeling the brown paper bag he had tucked there. He took a deep breath and pushed off the ground with his bum hand.

He never even heard the rattle. A sharp burning pain bit into his hand. He yelled and watched the snake slither from the bush next to him and disappear into the other shrubbery spread throughout the lot. Blood dripped from the puncture wounds, his hand already beginning to swell. He quickly took off the brace and threw it on the ground. *Well, I'll be damned*, he thought and couldn't do anything but laugh. And laugh. He laughed so hard he cried, slumped against the brick. Weeping. He let out a scream. One of pain and of frustration and anger. Rage pulsed through his face, and he picked himself off the ground and crossed the street. *If it wasn't for bad luck.*

"Jackie!" Dan yelled his name over and over again until the two thugs appeared in the hall and asked him what the hell he was doing there. Dan told them to go fuck themselves, that he was there to see Jackie. The two men led him by the armpits into the same damp room as before, as musty and miserable as ever. The pain was growing tremendously in his arm, and he felt nauseous. Sweat beading along his hairline. Jackie burst through the door like he always did, and the sound of rust scraping the concrete filled the room. Dan tried to stay focused, feeling his vision blur. Jackie multiplied and stood next to himself.

"Did you find the person responsible?" Jackie said.

Dan reached into his back pocket and pulled out the brown bag wrapped into a small brick, and threw it down at Jackie's feet.

"The fuck is this?" Jackie said.

"Ten grand. It's all the money I owe. I'm done. Give me my phone and leave me and Annie alone."

The damp air was filled with laughter from Jackie's two henchmen, really having at it. Jackie remained silent and rested his hands on his stomach. "You're not out of anything. I told you to find the person who did this. Until then, I own you. It was never about the money, kid. You think I give a fuck about ten grand? I'm sick of your smart mouth. I'm sick of all your schemes. And I'm sick of you. Plain and simple. You're done when I say you're done." The two men on each side of Jackie kept laughing. "Did you find who did that to my daughter?" He choked back emotion, clearing his throat sharply. "Broke her up like that?"

Dan looked at the man next to Jackie, the one with the eyebrows, the one who hurt Annie and wanted to do more to her. The one that put a gun in her mouth. Watching him laughing, thinking Jackie was so fucking funny all the time.

"I did," Dan said. The room got quiet in an instant. "But I don't think we should talk about it here." He looked at Eyebrows, then back to Jackie. "I think *just me and you* should talk about this. Without them."

"Goddamnit Dan! Tell me who killed my daughter!" A gun in his hand now, resting by his thigh.

Dan talked in a hushed tone, almost a whisper. "Jackie, I don't think you're getting what I'm saying." He looked over at Eyebrows again. "I think we need to discuss this," he paused, "away from *them*." Jackie's eyes bulged, and he slowly turned to his men.

"What the fuck," Eyebrows said and put his hands up toward Jackie.

"What's going on?" The other one said, his eyes darting between Jackie and Eyebrows.

"Did one of you—"

"Jackie, I have no idea what the *fuck* he is talking about. Why are you—don't look at me like that. I didn't—don't fucking listen to this guy!" Eyebrows voice in total panic.

Jackie's face turned bright red, and his cheeks trembled. He turned slowly back to Dan.

"Ask yourself, Jackie—think about it—and ask yourself if you ever saw anyone looking at her. Looking at her in a way that made you wonder. Saying weird stuff. Maybe about her looks, or the last time they saw her. *Think*."

Jackie turned back to Eyebrows. Murder in his eyes.

"Me? Jack, come on. I have no idea—*he's lying!*" Eyebrows said. He talked so fast his words tripped over themselves.

Dan's arm was killing him. His whole body hurt, and he couldn't stop sweating. He felt like he might throw up. "Someone got sick that night? When I brought her here. No one else did. Why?"

"Shut the fuck up!" Eyebrows pulled his gun and pointed it at Dan. Dan flinched and ducked, curling into a ball on the ground. The room filled with gunshots. One after the other, some in unison, overlapping. The sound broke Dan's eardrums again, and he could only hear buzzing. Echoes ricocheted off each wall, colliding and bouncing again. The air smelled of copper and gunpowder, and when Dan opened his eyes, both men were dead on the ground, and Jackie was holding his hand over his stomach. His shirt red and wet under his palm. Jackie coughed blood onto his fist and walked over to the wall, leaning then sliding down, landing with a thud when his legs gave out. Slumped over on the cold cement, breathing heavy and labored.

The excitement made Dan's heart race, and now he felt like death. Blinking his eyes into focus, completely covered in sweat. He looked over at the two bodies lying there and walked to the package of money. He picked it up and went over to Jackie. Dan slid down the wall next to him, resting his head against the brick.

"You think you're going to die?" Dan said, his eyes closed, trying to focus on his breathing.

"Seems like it," Jackie said, looking straight ahead, his voice weak. He started to cough, his chest rattling.

"I can't say I'm sorry to hear it."

Jackie let out a short, unexpected laugh. "Didn't think you would be." He coughed more blood into his fist. "This really hurts."

The two sat side by side in silence on the wall, listening to the deafening ringing of the room. Jackie broke it, softly.

"I'm scared, Dan," he said.

Dan was focused on staying conscious. "Me too, Jack. Me too."

"You think this is how my little girl felt?"

Dan remained quiet. Far off in his mind. Pain pulsing through his body. Focusing on staying conscious. He thought of Annie.

"Dan—"

"*Hmm?*"

"You remember that girl from science class? She fucked the teacher. It was all over school."

"Arabella Kingsman."

"She was the first girl I was ever with. You know that?"

"I remember hearing that back in the day, yeah."

"I might have loved her. Her middle name was Lydia," Jackie said.

He waited for Dan to say something, but nothing came out.

"I wonder what she's up to after all this time," Jackie said.

"If you survive this, maybe hit her up."

"That's a good idea." Jackie looked at Dan's hand from the corner of his eye, unable to move his head. "That looks horrible." He coughed again. "I did all of that?"

"Mostly. I got bit by a rattler, too," Dan said, holding his hand. Swollen and discolored.

"When?"

"Right outside, just now."

Jackie started laughing. The laughter grew until the coughing started, wet and loud and violent. He winced, grabbing his stomach. "Fuck," Jackie said and wiped the blood from his hand onto his pants. "You have the worst luck of anyone I ever met."

"Don't I know it," Dan said, and laid the brick of cash on Jackie's lap. "Here you go."

"Keep it, I don't want it."

"No, I'm paid in full. We're square."

Jackie spit blood onto the ground. "Square."

Dan stood up and searched through Jackie's pockets, Jackie too weak to fight it. He picked up his cellphone, put it in his pocket, and placed the dead man's phone in Jackie's hand.

"You want me to call an ambulance?"

Jackie softly shook his head back and forth. "I'll be okay, get out of here."

"Take care, Jack," he said. "If you live, maybe don't be such an asshole with the rest of your life."

"Dan?"

He stopped in the doorway and turned.

"Frank really did that to my little girl?"

"You asked me to find the man who did it, and I did." He looked at the two men on the ground, all the life oozing from them onto the floor. "Sorry it turned out this way."

Jackie said something, but Dan didn't hear.

The sun and heat punched Dan in the face and split his head like a log—pain surging through every molecule of his body. Dan braced himself on the wall and vomited onto the ground, needing all his strength to keep himself from falling into it. He staggered to the car and sat behind the wheel, leaning his head back against the headrest. Shutting his eyes tight, then opening them wide. Trying to force the blurring into the background again. He leaned over and opened the glove box, pulling out the snakebite kit Annie left in there. Dan ripped at the plastic with his teeth. He popped open the kit like a pill and dug out the razor. Trembling, he cut a deep X between the puncture wounds. Too exhausted to yell, he used the suction cup on the cut, pulling blood from the wound, hoping he was getting some venom from it, too. He opened the door and vomited one last time before he started the car. He opened the window and blasted the radio, anything he could think of to keep him alert as he drove.

Little lizards ran across the road, and the flatness of the asphalt looked like liquid as the heat rose. It was a beautiful day, with the sky so vividly blue and the clouds white like cotton. It was hard to believe that what just happened didn't affect the weather. Dan expected it to be raining and miserable when he left Jackie's, sludging through the mud and flooded streets—but it was as calm and clear as any regular day. Dan tried to stay focused on the road. He had to get to the hospital. He knew that if he remained on this stretch long enough, and if he could stay awake and not go into shock, that he would get there. He just needed to stay focused. And he knew Annie was at the hotel, and that the hotel was on the way to the hospital. That was lucky, he thought.

And it was about time he had a touch of good luck.

Acknowledgments

The first time I tried writing this it was long. Long long. Short story length. Then I did another pass and trimmed it by over three thousand words—and it was still short story length. Then it occurred to me that what I have to say about the people here will always be infinite. Words will always fail me. So if that's the case, I probably don't need to use all of them all at once.

To **Jess**, the impossibility of threading the needle between *'all the stars in the firmament would burn out before I ran out of words to express my love'* and *'you're cool, thanks for marrying me'* is real. There is no me without you. You're my other glove, my other torch, and my other penny crushed into one. No one keeps me grounded more. If I were to summarize all of that into three words, they would be: *Shantay, you stay.*

ACKNOWLEDGMENTS

Kevin. The last time you came over, you handed me a butterfly-knife and a book by Albert Camus, and I'm hard pressed to think of anything more fitting. You've been the MVP of getting this book out and this indie press started. It couldn't have been done without you. Thanks for helping me create dangerously. Two sides, one coin.

Matty and **Jon**, you guys are the constant roots that keep me from spiraling. You keep me sharp and inspired. I would be completely lost without you. Few people are ever blessed with a friendship like this. I really lovzzZZzzZzz, sorry I bored myself, what was I saying?

Mom, **Jen**, and **Harmony** (who is never ever allowed to read this book, ever. You'll never be old enough), thank you for your endless love and support, memories, and laughs—which are usually at one of our expenses. We make a hell of a team!

Lanie, you've read this book in different drafts, and here it is in its final form. I hope you like it. Thank you for being the best mother-in-law in existence! How'd I ever get so lucky? That time we were snowed in and watched endless Arrested Development has been the pinnacle of relaxation I've been chasing ever since!

Dolores, thank you for your support and encouragement. You accepted me into your family without a second thought and with open arms. I can't imagine anything stopping you from reading this, although I'm sure Lanie and Jess will try! But knowing you'll read this, all I can do is say...*sorry! Ugh, I never account for my grandma reading what I write! Oops!*

ACKNOWLEDGMENTS

William Boyle, the bulk of why my other iterations of acknowledgments failed was because when it comes to you and Jimmy, the words don't ever stop. I've kicked around starting a small press for maybe twenty years, and you've been encouraging it from the jump. Your support in writing and life is immeasurable. You introduced me to so many of my favorite things and artists who've staked a foothold in all of my work. As I said, I could go on forever, but I won't. From where I'm sitting I don't see how *any* of this is possible without you. I know *"fail again, fail better"* isn't a Bill Boyle original, but you shared it with me, and it changed everything. There's not enough thanks in the world, boyo.

Jimmy Cajoleas, man, where do I even begin? You took this book from scraps to what it is now. The lessons and edits you showed me still carry on in my writing and life—*"You have to make it matter to people who don't give a shit"* is more than plotting advice, it's how to navigate day-to-day life. You put up with my endless questions and ADHD-riddled emails and texts so long our phones need to nap between sending them. You know how this book started, and here it is now! I hope it makes you proud, man. Thank you for everything you did and all the things you didn't even know you were doing.

Jeffery Dein. Sir, what can I say? The reason all my writing reads like my first Bible teacher was also the first person to show me Fargo when I was thirteen is because that's exactly what happened. It's the line I always tap dance on. The first film festival we ever entered together I got us DQ'd because of the cursing in it—look at me now! You might possibly be the most important person to have ever entered my life. Everything changed, and there's no looking back, nor do I ever want to. *Love you, miss you, bye.*

Bob Kaplan—drop the vernacular! Like with most things, it takes a village to put out a book, and there hasn't been a villager more involved. You help me edit, bounce ideas, offer lines and tweaks, play devil's advocate when needed. You keep me afloat when I'm spiraling. You make office days easier and remind me of all the good things outside the prison walls when I can't see them myself. There's zero chance this book gets published without you. I'm blessed to have you as such a good friend. And Senior Copy Editor!

Doug Powers. Twilight Zone, W.C. Fields, and a mouth that fires faster than it aims! I guess we have an aesthetic, huh? You're in the same league as Mr. Dein, where you balance on this line of dad, brother, and friend—I don't fully get the breakdown, but I love every moment. I'm glad I'll always have an audience for my "Ed Wynne as Ricky Roma" impression, because Lord knows Jess can't stand it. Thank you for all the laughs, talks, and all of the once-in-a-lifetime concerts you've taken me to! Can't wait to have you back in New York.

Travis, **Argenis**, **Helen**, and **Angela**, thank you for making weekdays more manageable and less...*toaster-bathbomby*. I wouldn't be able to grind it out without you. Ang, you're the best to ever do it! Keep going! Trav, you're the...*okay*ist to ever do it, so you can just stop.

ACKNOWLEDGMENTS

Sean, we used to text each other lines for future stories and songs so we didn't forget them—and now we're here. Not too shabby. Thank you for your nonstop friendship and encouragement, and for understanding melancholy more than anyone else I know. It makes navigating life much easier with someone in the trenches with me.

God, wrapping this up is rough! **Michelle**, you're a true blue day one, and have been reading all my stuff since we were kids—good and bad. Nothing's changed much these days, and I'm thankful we've been at each other's sides through everything life has thrown at us—good and bad. Glad we don't have to go it alone. Thank you to **Josh Dyke** who gets me in ways no one else really can. And to **Joelle Dyke** who is so great she makes Josh look like shit. Thanks to **Aaron Weiss**, you once wrote that I resurrected Hemingway—I don't know if I can, but fingers crossed this book is a start! **Megan Abbott**, thank you for your friendship, advice, and being a partner in grief. And thank you for writing *End of Everything*—that changed a lot for me. Thank you to **Lynne Nardella**, whose insight and ideas helped shape this book, and whose friendship helped shape the characters. *Brian Nardella forever!* Thank you to **Liz**, **Anna**, **Danielle**, and **Nicole**, whose voices are all throughout this story. Thank you to **Stanton McCaffery** and the crew of **Rock and a Hard Place**; one hell of a great community that publishes great work! (I even added a semicolon just for you.)

And to **everyone I couldn't fit here**, and **everyone reading**: Thank you, let's hope this is the first of many.

www.ingramcontent.com/pod-product-compliance
Lightning Source LLC
Chambersburg PA
CBHW020912310726
48980CB00011B/850/J

* 9 7 9 8 9 9 9 7 7 7 4 0 9 *